A second shot threw dirt up into his face and he crabbed sideways, trying to get out of the line of fire. Four explosions coming in rapid succession followed his path, marking it with rising dust clouds, forcing Jubal to realize that the hidden marksman held him under a clear field of fire.

Then a shout brought a curse to his lips.

"Cade! I told you I'd get you. You're dead meat."

Somewhere out in the brush Kincaid was stalking him with a Winchester. . . .

Drawn to a lawless mining town in the blistering plains of New Mexico, Jubal Cade embarks upon a grisly vendetta—to hunt down and kill his wife's scarfaced murderer. But the gun-toting medico gets more than he bargained for as he finds himself dodging Apaches and leading a manhunt to avenge THE GOLDEN DEAD.

Also by Charles R. Pike

# The Golden Dead

Charles R. Pike

CHELSEA HOUSE
New York, London
1980

Copyright © 1980 by Chelsea House Publishers, a division of
Chelsea House Educational Communications, Inc.
All rights reserved
First published in Great Britain in 1976 by Granada Publishing Limited
Printed and bound in the United States of America
LC: 80-69219
ISBN: 0-87754-236-8


Chelsea House Publishers
Harold Steinberg, Chairman & Publisher
Andrew E. Norman, President
Susan Lusk, Vice President

A Division of Chelsea House Educational Communications, Inc.
70 West 40 Street, New York 10018

# CHAPTER ONE

From the shelter of the ridge the waiting men could see him coming, a small figure huddled down into his faded duster against the blowing Arizona wind. He hunched in his saddle, face tilted downwards to avoid the burning sand, his right hand resting on his hip, close to the butt of the saddle-mounted rifle.

He was letting the horse pick its own way up the canyon trail, not paying too much attention to his surroundings. That was his first mistake.

His second came when the arrow thudded into his left thigh. Instead of kicking the horse into a gallop that might have taken him to safety, he yelled at the sudden pain, involuntarily hauling the animal's head round as he groped at the feathered shaft protruding from his leg. The pony skittered around in a circle, sensing panic and picking up the raw contagion of fear. Its eyes rolled and it began to buck as it caught the stink of fear-sweat from the rider.

Up on the ridge the waiting men laughed in anticipation. They had been stretched out in the sun for the better part of two hours, and they were bored: the lone rider offered a diversion. Lazily, taking it in turns, they rose up and sighted on the target. A Winchester bullet ploughed through the horse's neck, bringing the animal down in a cloud of dust and snorted blood. Immediately afterwards, three arrows sprouted from the rider's chest, knocking him backwards off the falling horse.

He hit the dry river-bed with a grunt of pain and surprise, but he held the rifle in his right hand. And as two more arrows hit his mount's ribs, he triggered a shot that killed the animal instantaneously, providing him with a degree of cover.

Painfully, he pulled himself up against the corpse, taking care to rest on his side so that the arrows would not rip through the fragile shell of his chest.

Firing at random, he blasted four shots towards the ridge.

None found a target and the waiting men grinned as the bullets fountained plumes of sand upwards into the afternoon sky. Then they fired a volley that ripped apart the carcase of the dead horse, bullets ploughing through the body to blind the lone defender as they threw sand up into his face.

One, at least, hit him, smashing ribs as it tore into his body. He screamed and spat blood and sighted his rifle with the cold fury of a man who knows he is going to die and wants only to take as many enemies as he can with him down the lonely road to oblivion.

His bullet hit square between the eyes of a painted face, mashing the broad, flat nose to a bloody pulp as it tore the brain behind to ragged shreds. The Apache sat back, dropping his bow as his hands lost their feeling and his long black hair fluttered out from his skull as the .30 calibre shell exploded through the rear of his cranium. Fragments of bone, coloured blood-red and smeared with grey brain matter spumed over the man next to him.

'Shit!' He was a white man, dressed in dirty Levis and a sun-bleached checked shirt. 'Damn' injuns never could keep their head in a fight.'

He wiped bloody slime from his face and drew a careful bead on the solitary figure below.

'All right, mister. One right where it hurts.'

It was the last thing he ever said, because a bullet hit his chest as he lifted up to sight his Winchester. It hit him dead centre in the breastbone, ricochetting off his spine to spiral downwards through his stomach and exit from his belly. He slumped forward into the sand of the ridge, Winchester unfired as a spreading pool of bright crimson puddled out beneath him.

Beside him a man with a long scar running across his forehead shouted at the other ambushers.

'Natchez, Morgan. Get the hell around that wash. Take him from behind.'

'OK, Kincaid,' grunted the dark man called Morgan. 'We're on our way. Let's go, injun.'

The two men, one white and one red, began to belly their way along the ridge, working out from the field of fire. Carefully, they made for a curve in the river and wriggled across to come up the far side where they stood up and began to run for the high ground. They made the far ridge and started to work down towards the man sprawled behind the dead pony. They moved silently as their companions put down covering fire, biding their time in anticipation of the kill until they held the man under clear sight.

Then they opened fire.

One bullet took the man beneath the left shoulder, hurling him forward against the horse. The second ripped through his right elbow, knocking the rifle from his grasp. As he reached out with his remaining good hand to seize the weapon, Natchez placed a shell in the small of his back.

The man arched over, head nearly touching his boots, twisted to one side and died, his heels drumming a brief farewell to life as it flooded from his body.

Morgan put two more shots into the corpse, just to be sure, and called across the wash.

'Got him, Kincaid. He's about as dead as he can be.'

Over the ridge, Kincaid rose to his feet and shouted back.

'So let's see what he's got.'

Like vultures descending on a fresh carcase, the mixed group of Apaches and white men went down to the corpse. They stripped the dead man of his guns and ammunition, pulled off his boots, dragged off his clothes and ransacked his saddlebags.

When they rode off all that remained was a naked body, minus scalp, and a dead horse with no saddle.

Morgan complained about the meagre pickings.

Kincaid grinned, his cold black eyes boring into the other man, so that the words dried up in his mouth. He was scared of Kincaid.

'Beats workin', don't it? Take the handout an' don't get doleful about it.'

# CHAPTER TWO

'It's one almighty hell of a mess.' The speaker was a small, fair man dressed in a neat pinstripe with a drummer's sample case resting across the tidily-pressed trousers of his cheap suit. 'Good old Crook drove the Apaches out of the Mogallons so the whole Salt River territory got opened up fer minin'. The diggers moved in an' hit paydirt an' the next thing they knew the Apaches were back. Only this time they was better organized an' riding with a bunch of renegade whites. I had a good trade goin' up there along the river. Now it's too damn' dangerous. A man never knows how long he'll keep his hair.'

He brushed absent-mindedly at the sparse blond strands pomaded across his skull and eyed the man sitting beside him. He had chosen his companion because the other man looked as though he might be a drummer, too. He was nothing much to look at, a slim, dark-haired man with deep-set brown eyes that looked as though they had seen too much grief. A well-cut, but obviously worn, suit of grey cloth matched by a battered grey derby, and a travel-marked black valise. He looked like one more of America's travelling salesmen, peddling his cheap wares around the cow towns that marked the route of the Atchison, Topeka and Santa Fe line from west of the Missouri to the Great Divide.

The only incongruous note about him was the lever-action Spencer propped against the seat close to his right hand.

If the drummer had been a little more observant, he might have noticed the slight bulge on the left side of Jubal Cade's jacket, where the converted .30 calibre Colt rested in its custom-made shoulder holster. If he had been less interested in his own troubles, he might have seen the cold uninterest in Jubal's eyes.

Because he wasn't and felt lonely, he carried on talking.

'Yeah. I had a good trade in patent medicines goin' on up there. There's a whole damn' town sprung up an' no doctor to tend miners with busted legs an' the like.'

'That right?' Jubal showed interest for the first time.

'You better believe it,' averred the drummer. 'There's the better part of a thousand dirt-grubbers workin' the length of the Salt River. They got a town goin' that numbers a few hundred head with stores an' saloons to rook the dust out of their pokes an' sweet little else.'

Jubal studied the garrulous trader carefully, calculating how far he could rely on the information. Since boarding the train at Topeka in the hope that the change from the Kansas Pacific line would put Ben Agnew's hired killers off his trail* he had been wondering where his next buck would come from. The bulk of his funds remained in St. Louis, security against the continuing care of Andy Prescott at the Lenz Clinic, and he needed money. Now it sounded like his boring companion might have put him on the right track.

'Tell me more,' he smiled pleasantly.

'Hell,' grinned the drummer, pleased to have woken a spark of interest in his taciturn travelling mate, 'it's wide open. Providing a man's prepared to risk gettin' his skull shot off. I ain't.'

'But you said the Army cleared the Indians,' Jubal prompted.

'I said Crook drove 'em onto the reservations,' grunted the drummer. 'I also said some came back with a whole pack of new friends. Not to mention repeating rifles an' a sudden passion for pure banditry.'

He paused to swig from a medicine bottle extracted from his case, offering the dark fluid to Jubal.

'No thanks,' Jubal grinned, 'I don't feel in need of medication.'

'Medication, hell!' replied the drummer. 'This here's half straight whiskey an' half coloured water. Fetches a dollar a bottle along the Salt River.' He capped the mixture and laughed. 'I been sellin' it to the miners for everything from snake-bite to sunburn.'

He paused as a regretful look passed briefly over his face.

'An' now the whole thing's closed down because of the raiders.'

'But there's no doctor up there?' Jubal made the question sound casual. 'Seems to me a man could pick up a tidy stake if

* See – Jubal Cade: The Burning Man

he sold the right medicines and maybe dug a little on the side.'

The drummer snorted. 'Right. He could. Trouble is, he'd be liable to wind up dead while he was doin' it.'

Jubal nodded and sank back into the silence that had marked his passage from St. Louis through to Trinidad. Most of the journey had been spent worrying about Andy and the validity of Ben Agnew's promise that the boy would remain apart from their personal feud*, but the thought that, whatever the final outcome of the operation might be, money would be necessary to Andy's education and care was never far from Jubal's consciousness. Now, out of the blue, the talkative con-man sitting beside him seemed to offer a solution. If there was a mining town along the Salt River that needed a doctor, there was no reason why Jubal Cade should not supply the service. And if there was gold to be found in the Sierra Mogallon, there was no reason why he should not try to dig some out. Either way, it sounded like a good place to hide out for a while.

He made polite noises while the drummer went on talking, not listening as he came to a swift decision.

When the train stopped in Santa Fe, Jubal refused an invitation to share a room with the salesman and set out to locate a stable.

He found a livery outfit two blocks down from the depot and blew one third of his remaining money on a big-chested pinto and a worn saddle. It was early afternoon and he spent the rest of it stocking up his medical bag and the supplies he figured on using during his journey to the Salt River. He was by no means sure that he was doing the right thing, but – he reassured himself – he had once heard about a man down in Texas who had walked into a crazy war between some Mexican peasants and a gang of bandits simply because it seemed like a good idea at the time. That man, Jubal heard, came out alive. Maybe he would come out richer.

Either way, he was committed; he had only sufficient money left to book into a cheap hotel for the night, stock up on cartridges and buy a bottle of whiskey. He decided against the last, preferring to keep his remaining few dollars against the time when he might really need them.

* See – Jubal Cade: Double Cross

Early the next morning he headed out for the Rio Grande, splashing through the shallows in the late afternoon to make camp in New Mexico. He saw no-one in the wide, dusty land; there were no homesteads, no ranches, no sign of life other than the prairie dogs and occasional coyotes skittering away from the pinto's hooves. The night was desert-cold and even the boiling coffee he brewed over a brushwood fire failed to take the chill from his bones. He woke stiff and grateful for the chance to ease the numbing coldness from his bones in the long ride towards San Rafael. There, at least, he could find a warm saloon and, maybe, a game of poker.

The town was the better part of a hundred miles to the south-west and Jubal made three more stops before he came in sight of the ragged string of timber buildings lying in a bowl formed by the New Mexican uplands. A single, rutted trail led into the place past a weathered signpost that bore the legend: Welcome to San Rafael. Jubal could just about decipher the faded letters as he walked his pony towards the solitary street.

He rode in slow and easy. Too often in the past these tiny tank towns had erupted into sudden, unexpected violence. Briefly, he remembered a place called Iberia, where he had seen his wife killed as he stood in helpless anguish*. The memory etched lines of pain deep into his face and at the thought of the scarfaced man who had slaughtered Mary, his lips compressed beneath eyes that blazed with sudden fury. Jubal had promised himself that he would kill the man and the past months had been occupied with the lonely search for vengeance.

With a conscious effort he pushed the ghosts of the past from his mind and concentrated on the town sprawled before him.

It was smaller than Iberia, a straggle of one- and two-storey wooden buildings flanking a dusty street. He spotted a sun-bleached hotel standing beside a saloon, a general store and, at the far end of the street, a livery stable. That was about the full extent of the town, although a handful of ramshackle houses, some sporting attempts at gardens, indicated that people actually lived here.

Jubal wondered what they did in this God-forsaken desert

* See – Jubal Cade: The Killing Trail

11

country. Not very much, to judge by the loafers sprawled in tilted chairs along the boardwalk. He grinned ruefully as he headed for the stable, the hope of a poker game was receding fast and with it his chance to increase the fistful of dollars in his pocket.

A freckle-faced youngster grabbed his bridle as he reached the entrance of the stable and Jubal dropped gratefully to the ground.

'Feed and water her, will you?' he asked. 'Go easy on the water. We came a long way and I aim to ride out tomorrow.'

'Sure thing, mister,' grinned the boy. 'Make it a round dollar and I'll curry her too.'

'You do that, son,' Jubal agreed. 'I'll be by tomorrow and pay you then. OK?'

'Sure. Tonight she'll bed down better'n you.'

Jubal untied his medical bag from the saddle, slid the Spencer from its scabbard and began to walk slowly back down the street. He was aware of the townsfolk watching him, sensing eyes that peered from windows in addition to the overt stares of the men lining the boardwalk. He wondered if it was because San Rafael saw too few strangers, or some other reason that prompted their curiosity. Either way, pure habit curled his trigger finger around the hair-fine action of the Spencer, his thumb hooking casually over the hammer. He hefted the familiar weight in his right hand, letting the muzzle droop downwards so that, should he need to use it, the rifle's blast would lift the barrel.

Nothing happened, however, as he paced the creaking boards to the entrance of the hotel.

He pushed through the door and found himself in what might once have been a respectable establishment. Now the velvet plush was faded from the banquette chairs placed around the foyer, flies buzzed around his head and when he dropped his valise onto a handy chair, a cloud of dust lifted up into the sultry air.

He walked over to the desk.

'I want a room and a bath. And if you got a restaurant I'll take dinner.'

The man behind the desk woke with a start, his eyes flickering around the room as though he expected trouble rather than a client.

12

'Sure, sir. Let me just check the register.'

He began to paw at a dog-eared ledger that raised more dust than the chairs, squinting down at the yellowing pages as though he was having difficulty finding an empty room. Jubal waited patiently, allowing the clerk to carry out his charade.

Finally, the man looked up nervously.

'Reckon I can fit you into the first floor front,' he said quickly, as though he expected Jubal to argue. 'One o' the best we got.'

'Yeah?' Jubal's voice was even and serious. 'How much?'

'Two dollars?' The clerk's voice tailed off in a way that suggested he expected Jubal to refuse.

'Tell you what.' Jubal reached for his valise. 'Throw in that bath and I'll pay one dollar.'

'Food extra?'

'Yeah, food extra,' Jubal grinned as he took the key the clerk pushed across the counter, 'just get that bath ready.'

'Straight away, sir.' The man was simpering as Jubal headed for the stairs. 'But sir, you didn't sign the register.'

Jubal didn't turn.

'I know.'

He climbed the stairs and located the room. It was spacious for the price, carpeted in faded red with a large bed that sparked bright flashes off the brasswork, a closet and a washstand. The pitcher standing in the blue china bowl showed a green slime mark around the inside: it was obvious that the place had stood empty a long time.

Jubal dropped his valise on one side of the bed, propped the Spencer against the wall on the right hand side and stretched gratefully out on the coverlet. To his surprise, no dust rose from the thing. Maybe, he mused, San Rafael's lone hotel still held hopes of success. He grinned to himself and lay still for a few minutes. Deliberately, he allowed his muscles to relax, concentrating on the comfortable softness of the feather mattress as the travel aches eased from his body. It was hot and the air itself held a lassitude that prompted drowsiness to the extent that he was slipping down into sleep when a pounding on the door brought him to his feet in a single lithe movement, the shoulder-holstered Colt appearing suddenly in his right hand.

He walked softly to the door and pulled it open, the long barrel of the handgun prodding forward.

13

In the corridor, the desk clerk jumped back, waving his hands as though to fend off the gun.

'Bath,' he stuttered. 'It's ready.'

'Thanks.' Jubal's grin calmed the man a little so that he stood still as Jubal lowered the gun. 'Where is it?'

'Two doors down. Hot water's ready an' I put towels out.'

He backed away, still nervous, and scurried down the stairs. Jubal watched him go, wondering again why the people of San Rafael were so jumpy. He shrugged, dismissing the thought; after all, he wasn't planning to stay longer than a day.

He locked the door of his room and headed for the bath. The place was steamy and relaxing, the big tin tub inviting after the days and nights on the trail. Swiftly, he shucked out of his suit, hanging the shoulder holster on a peg, handy beside the tub, and slid into the welcoming water. He lay there for a long time before he began to scrub the saddle sweat from his body. Then he soused himself with the buckets of cold water left by the clerk and climbed out of the tub. Towelled dry and dressed again, he went back to the room. It was getting on for evening and he decided to check out the saloon before eating, but before going out he went over the Colt, cleaning the big gun and loading the chambers with fresh cartridges. Then he pushed it into the holster and walked down to the street.

Outside, the air was still heavy, the brooding quiet of late afternoon settling over the town like a pall. In this desert country there was something ominous about the impending night. Or maybe, Jubal reminded himself, it was just something about San Rafael itself.

Either way, the same loafers who had watched him enter the hotel watched him leave with the same wary interest. He could feel their eyes on his back as he pushed open the bat-wing doors of the saloon and stepped inside. It was cooler there, dark and shuttered against the sun, the spigot of the beer tap inviting in the gloom. Three men looked up from a desultory game of stud as Jubal crossed the sawdusted floor to the long bar, his eyes casually — but carefully — checking his surroundings.

For once there was no encircling balcony, just a low ceiling, the bar and a scattering of chairs and tables. Apart from the one occupied by the card players, only two others were being

14

used. One was occupied by two men who looked like cowhands, the other by a tall, moustached man wearing the beat-up trousers of a black suit with matching vest. Pinned to the chest was a tarnished brass star.

As Jubal ordered his beer, the man rose and walked slowly over.

'We don't get too many strangers here,' he murmured as he joined Jubal.

'That a fact?' Jubal's grin was open and pleasant.

'It's a fact. San Rafael's kinda off the beaten track. Folks who don't live here are either passin' through or on their way someplace else.'

Jubal sipped his beer, appreciating the coldness of it before he replied.

'Meaning you'd like to know why I'm here?'

'Somethin' like that.' The lawman eyed the small figure beside him, noting the faded suit and grey derby. And the way Jubal used his left hand to raise the beer glass.

'Well, I'm just passing through,' said Jubal easily, 'heading for the Salt River.'

'Bad country, that,' grunted the marshal. 'Lot o' trouble down there since they found the gold.'

He shrugged, letting his gaze wander over the near-empty saloon.

'This used to be quite a town. Then they hit gold an' most folks upped and left, figgerin' to come back rich. Ain't none come back yet.'

'That why it's so quiet?' Jubal asked.

'That's about the size of it,' agreed the officer, 'the gold fever hit this town hard.'

Jubal didn't say anything. He was waiting for the marshal to explain why one lone stranger should arouse such interest in a town nearly deserted by its population. The lawman took the silent hint.

'Thing is,' he said quietly, 'every so often we get a few people comin' through lookin' fer relaxation an' the like. Miners, gamblers; that kind. When they hit San Rafael they get kinda disappointed. Some o' them try to take it out on the town. I hope you ain't one.'

'Don't worry,' Jubal paused to order a second beer, 'I'm not.

15

Like I said: I'm just passing through. Come tomorrow I'll be gone.'

He swallowed the amber liquid and turned away, conscious of the marshal watching him as he left the saloon. Outside, the sudden desert night had come down like a warm black shutter. It was too early yet for the chill to have set in and cicadas were chirruping as lanterns flared behind dusty window panes. Jubal paused, savouring the quiet for a moment before entering the hotel.

He caught the smell of cooking and followed his nose to a room off to one side of the reception area. As he pushed the door open he saw the clerk, a tired-looking woman who might once have been attractive, and three other men seated around a big, circular table. A sixth place was set, so Jubal took it, hanging his derby on a peg alongside the door as he ducked his head in general greeting.

The woman appeared to be in charge of the kitchen, for she rose as Jubal smiled at her and walked through a side door. The other diners grunted in reply to his greeting and went on eating.

Conversation remained at a minimum as Jubal forked up burnt beans and overdone steak and after a while he gave up and ate in silence. Once again, he was conscious of the nervousness in the air, noting the surreptitious glances the other men threw his way. The clerk and the woman ignored everyone, eating hurriedly and leaving the table before the guests were finished. Jubal drained his coffee cup, murmured his farewell, and left the dining room.

Outside, the air was cold, stars sparkling in a clear sky like watching eyes. Jubal shivered and stepped into the saloon. The marshal was still there, playing cards now with a fair-haired man in worn levis and a sweat-stained shirt, and a plump, balding man dressed in a frayed brown suit.

He looked up as Jubal walked over to the bar. 'Care to make a fourth, stranger?'

'Why not?' Jubal relished the thought of a game.

He ordered a whiskey and joined the card players.

As he suspected, they were inexpert and he quickly took control of the game, using his natural talent to scoop in the small pots that built up. On fifty cent bets the winnings were never very big, but after two hours Jubal was twenty dollars in credit and the other players ready to quit. He took a final pot of five dollars in a face-off with the marshal, beating a ten-high straight with a full house of aces and sevens.

The lawman threw down his cards and grinned ruefully.

'Stranger,' he said softly, 'I made a mistake when I invited you to sit in. What are you, anyway? A gambler?'

'No.' Jubal was pocketing the pile of notes and coins. 'I'm a doctor.'

'A doctor!' Surprise registered on the man's face. 'I never seen a doctor so good at poker. Come to that, I ain't never seen a doctor wearin' a shoulder rig.'

Jubal glanced down at the slight bulge in his jacket where the rebuilt Colt hung in its holster.

'That's a long story,' he grinned, showing his broken front teeth, 'man down in Texas persuaded me to carry it*.'

'Buy you a drink?' The marshal pushed his chair away from the table. 'I'd kinda like to hear that story.'

Jubal had no particular desire to recount the events that had taken him to Laredo and the bloody confrontation with Roberto Blanco and Lee Kincaid. The memory of the scarfaced killer of his wife was still too fresh in his mind. But none the less, he did not wish to antagonize another lawman: Les Riley had proven difficult enough. So, briefly, he explained the origins of the Colt, holding back those parts of the story too personal to be comfortable in the telling.

The marshal – Longridge, Jubal learned, was his name – listened attentively, sipping his whiskey as Jubal spoke. When the smaller man had finished, he nodded once and turned away from the bar to stare directly at Jubal.

'Sounds to me, Cade, like trouble follows you around. Reckon it'd be a good thing if you rode on come mornin'.'

'I already told you,' Jubal replied, 'that's exactly what I aim to do.'

He turned on his heel and walked away, leaving Longridge to brood over the uneasy peace of his dying town.

Now that the night was drawing on, San Rafael seemed more like a ghost town than ever. The loafers were gone from the street and most of the houses stood in darkness. Apart from a couple of faint-lit windows, the only illumination came from

* See – Jubal Cade: Killer Silver

17

the kerosene lanterns in the saloon, their pale glow throwing shifting shadows out around Jubal as he headed for the hotel.

By the light of a single lantern he located his room key and went up to bed.

# CHAPTER THREE

The sun didn't seem to come up the next morning. Instead, a grey wash of falling rain obscured a pale glow in the sky, churning the sand of the main street to a muddy yellow froth. Jubal cursed as he splashed water in his face: if the storm kept up he would have to blow some of his poker money on a weatherproof.

He shaved quickly, dressed and went down to the dining room. Eggs, bacon and coffee were waiting with a basket of hot biscuits and no sign of the other guests. Jubal piled a plate with food and sat down to eat. Through the grimy window he watched the rain falling, wondering what kind of time he could make on his southward journey with the trail near washed out by the downpour. It would be hard going for both man and horse, but there was no reason to hang around San Rafael.

He finished breakfast, paid his bill, and walked out, valise in one hand, the Spencer in the other. Hugging the sidewalk to avoid the driving rain, he moved towards the livery stable.

When he came to the general store he went in, savouring the aroma of cured meats, dried goods and leather. A wizened old man appeared in the space left between two sides of smoked ham, blew a cloud of acrid cigar smoke over the meat, and asked Jubal what he wanted.

The odour of the storekeeper's cheap cigar reminded Jubal that he was fresh out of cheroots. They were one of the few luxuries he permitted himself and now he felt a sudden craving for the aromatic black tobacco.

'Cheroots, to start with,' he said, 'the smokeable kind.'

The storekeeper was by now puffing his own black tube close under Jubal's nose and the smell was overpowering.

'Right,' rasped the oldster, 'I got the best smokes this side o' Santa Fe. Two cents through to dollar seegars.'

He began to haul boxes out from under the counter, opening the lids so that Jubal could survey the contents. After several minutes spent sniffing the tobacco and checking the prices, Jubal selected a boxful that cost him two dollars. Then he

19

turned to the racks of clothing spaced against the far wall. In amongst the levis and shirts he spotted a rack of full-length coats, yellow dusters hanging next to darker weatherproofs.

He selected a dark blue storm coat that looked like it would fit and shrugged it on. It had been a good guess: the coat fitted as though it had been tailored to his size. Of heavy gaberdine, it hung down to his ankles, a big overlay protecting his shoulders like a cloak. The pockets on the hip were cut so that he could reach through to his jacket, allowing for easy access to the Colt on his shoulder, while buckles sewn on the outside were designed to take a holster.

'Best damn' coat in the store,' announced the salesman, 'got it shipped in from the East. An' seein' as how you obviously need a coat, I'll let you have it for ten dollars.'

It was a reasonable price and Jubal handed over the money, shoving the box of cheroots into one of the capacious pockets. Then he walked out towards the stable.

The youngster had kept his promise. The pinto was freshly groomed and well-rested, snickering softly as Jubal lashed his valise onto the saddle and slid the Spencer into its scabbard. He threw a silver dollar to the grinning boy and led the pony towards the entrance.

The rain was still teeming outside, obscuring vision behind a pale grey curtain. San Rafael was an even sorrier-looking town in the storm and the one street was empty, the windows of the houses and business premises staring blankly, like empty eyes, onto the lonely roadway.

Then, as he mounted, Jubal spotted someone moving through the rain.

A tall figure, clad in a black oilskin, was walking purposefully towards the stable, a big, rain-slicked scattergun held across his chest. Jubal recognized Marshal Longridge beneath the broad-brimmed, dripping stetson.

He stood the pinto as the lawman approached, wondering what brought him out of doors in such weather. Longridge supplied the answer as he came up, bringing the shotgun to bear on Jubal's chest.

'Don't make no sudden moves, Cade!'

The threatening muzzles of the Remington emphasized his words.

'What's the trouble?' Jubal sat the pinto quietly, keeping both hands in full sight of Longridge, noting the cocked hammers and taut trigger-finger.

'I got to thinkin' about your story an' it kinda rang bells.' The marshal paused to shake water from his hat brim. 'So I checked through some dodgers. Seems like there was a marshal up around the Colorado territory put a poster out on you.'

Inwardly, Jubal cursed, tensing his body for the action he knew must explode soon.

Outwardly, he remained calm and placatory.

'A poster? On me?'

'Yeah,' grunted Longridge, 'lawman by the name o' Riley. Wanted you pretty bad. I figger to give you to him.'

'Marshal,' said Jubal quietly, 'that'd be kind of hard. Riley's dead. He got himself mixed up in an accident on a train.'*

Longridge looked worried for a moment, then made up his mind.

'Don't make no difference, Cade. A poster means there's a reward somewhere. All I gotta do is hold you until I find out where.'

'Longridge,' Jubal's voice was quieter, with an underlying threat of danger that prompted the lawman to steady the dripping shotgun, 'I told you once and I told you twice, I'm heading for the Salt River. Now you listen to my advice and let me ride out.'

'Like hell!' It was a snarl prompted by avarice. 'You're money on the hoof, Cade. Money I figger to collect.'

'Could be,' said Jubal in the same quiet, tired tone, 'that you'll collect more than you bargain for.'

As he spoke, he kuicked the pinto forward, swinging sideways in the saddle as the rested horse threw itself willingly into a full gallop.

It hit Longridge full on, hurling him backwards in a tumbling somersault as the twin barrels of the Remington blasted pellets across the sky. Jubal ignored the sudden pricking in his right shoulder as he let himself fall from the saddle, crashing down into the rain-sodden street. He rolled as he hit, closing his eyes against the splashing water and grating sand.

He came up on one knee as the pinto halted several paces down the street, the Spencer levelled and cocked on Longridge.

The marshal was swearing hideously as he clawed soaking

* See – Jubal Cade: Vengeance Hunt

21

dust from his eyes. His hat was gone in the fall and rain was streaming down his face. It looked almost as though he was weeping in frustration. Still, he came up on his feet, clawing for the .33 calibre Star single-action pistol holstered in his oilskin.

Jubal saw what the man was trying to do and shouted over the sound of the rain.

'Longridge! Don't act like a fool.' The marshal was still fumbling with the handgun. 'I got no quarrel with you. Drop the gun and I'll ride out.'

'Screw you, Cade.' Longridge snarled the words, greed governing his better senses. 'I'm gonna kill you.'

He pulled the Star out of his pocket and raised his arm. Jubal had no wish to kill the man; any more than he had a choice in the matter. The marshal was lifting the revolver and at that range he could hardly miss.

Jubal squeezed the trigger of the Spencer as Longridge's gun levelled on his chest.

Fired from only a few feet away, the .30 calibre rifle bullet flipped Longridge backwards through the rain. It entered his chest directly over the heart, ripping life from the organ as it ploughed its way through splintering bone and pulping flesh to exit in a gaping hole from beneath his left shoulder blade. The black surface of his oilskin slickened suddenly as crimson pumped out over the smooth surface. He was dead before he hit the sidewalk.

His own bullet whistled past Jubal's ear, fluttering wet black hair in its passage. Jubal rose to his feet as the marshal's lungs exhaled their last consignment of air and turned to his horse.

The sooner, he figured, he could get out of San Rafael, the better.

He swung up into the saddle, still holding the Spencer ready to fire, and drove the pony in a fast canter out of town. Behind him, people were gathering around the bloody body of the dead lawman. Jubal didn't look back. He was more concerned with the red drips splattering his face. He had been close enough to Longridge for the marshal's blood to spray over his derby and now the blood was dripping off as he rode.

'Hell,' he muttered to himself, 'as if raindrops falling on my head wasn't enough.'

22

# CHAPTER FOUR

Jubal made the best time he could on the journey south towards the Salt River, pushing his mount on hard through the driving rain and pausing only to check his backtrail for any sign of pursuers. The citizens of San Rafael, however, were either too indolent or too frightened to mount any pursuit. And in any event, he consoled himself as the rain blew into his face, the filthy weather would serve to cover his tracks as effectively as any device he might employ.

He huddled down in the saddle, shrugged the coat closer around him, and pushed on.

The rain kept up until the next morning. Jubal's camp that night was cold and wet, there was no chance of getting a fire going and the best shelter he could find was a stunted mesquite tree that spread gnarled branches a scant few feet above the soaking sand. He draped a tarpaulin over a branch to make a crude tent, wrapped the stormproof around himself and settled down to a fitful night's sleep. Coffee was out of the question and his only consolation was a cheroot, nursed in cupped hands against the wind that blew rainwater in under the flap of his makeshift shelter. Finally, he slept.

He awoke with the rising sun on his face, shining bright and clear so that steam rose from the ground around his camp. Jubal set swiftly about making a fire, no longer worried about pursuit and thirsty for fresh-brewed coffee. He set the mess tin he had packed to boil and fried up strips of bacon; after the long, wet night he was hungry, eating gratefully between sips of the steaming, black coffee.

When he had finished he scattered the ashes of the fire and rode on. The journey took him several days, but at last he sighted a high bluff with a river running by its foot. From the directions he had been given this had to be the Salt River canyon, so now all he had to do was follow the water until he reached the mining camp. He headed the pinto down the steep incline leading to the riverbank and pushed on south-west.

Two days' travel brought him to the town, if it could be

called that. He was by no means sure as he eyed the straggle of jerry-built hutments and dirty canvas that took the place of houses. Still, this was his destination and he had come too far to turn back now. Keeping one hand close to the sheathed Spencer, Jubal rode towards the settlement.

It was near empty and Jubal decided that, like most mining camps, it came alive only after dark, the inhabitants making the most of every available hour of daylight to work their claims.

Studying the place as he rode, he noticed four saloon tents, the biggest sporting a wooden front from which a huge square of canvas was draped to form a roof. About seven tents and crude huts sported red lanterns and roughly-painted invitations to sample the doubtful pleasures offered by the whores within. There were several supply tents offering everything from bullets to beds, and a wooden building, looking more solid than any other, that turned out to be the assay office and bank. But of sleeping quarters there was no sign.

A saloon, Jubal decided, was about the best place to get information, so he halted in front of the largest and walked in.

'Welcome to the Golden Nugget, stranger.'

The speaker was a small man, dressed all in black, who limped slightly as he walked towards Jubal from the rear of the tent.

'I'm Nolan, owner of this impressive establishment.' He waved his hand to indicate the interior of the tent. 'What'll you have? First one's on the house.'

'Thanks,' Jubal grinned, 'I'll take a beer.'

'Give the man a drink, Harry,' Nolan turned to the waiting barkeep, 'and pour a whiskey for me.'

When the drinks appeared, Nolan steered Jubal over to a table towards the back of the saloon. There were no other drinkers around, though a couple of faded women in shabby red dresses cut to expose a good deal of pallid flesh eyed Jubal speculatively.

'I like to keep up with the latest news,' announced Nolan when they had seated themselves, 'it pays off in this business.'

His shrewd grey eyes studied Jubal carefully.

'Don't get me wrong. I ain't prying, but, gee, information's a stock in trade.'

24

Jubal grinned and sipped his drink. 'Truth is,' he replied, 'I heard you might need a doctor up here, so I came looking.'

'We sure do.' Nolan seemed surprised. 'But I hadn't figured you for a doctor. A drummer maybe, but not a doc.'

'Fully trained and ready to work,' smiled Jubal. 'If I can find a place to operate in.'

Nolan thought for a moment.

'Look, doctor . . .' he paused.

'Cade,' Jubal answered the unspoken question, 'Jubal Cade.'

'Cade,' continued Nolan. 'I got an idea. There's sleeping quarters out back with plenty of room and fairly clean. Whyn't you work here? Most of the boys come by, and if they know there's a doctor in the house I reckon more'll come in. That way we both benefit.'

Jubal thought for a moment. It was an attractive proposition, offering work and a place to sleep. He made a fast decision and nodded his head.

'All right, Nolan, you're on.'

'Call me Fred,' Nolan grinned, extending his right hand.

They shook on the deal and Nolan called for whiskey. As Harry brought the drinks over one of the whores rose from her chair and came towards them. Her cheap scent, mingled with sweat, wrinkled Jubal's nostrils in distaste. The flabby breasts she thrust at him as she hung over the table prompted him to turn his head. He remembered his encounter with the girls of the Tyson Troupe and the bloody outcome of that meeting* and forced himself to smile.

'Buy a girl a drink, mister?' she wheedled.

Nolan had noticed Jubal's grimace and spoke before his companion could open his mouth to reply.

'Frankie, be an angel and go sit down. We got things to talk about.'

Frankie swore under her breath, looking angrily at the saloon's owner, but she obeyed the flat authority in his voice, flouncing back to the shadows at the far end.

'Beasts, ain't they?' Nolan murmured, 'but that's what folks want up here: pleasure, short and cheap.'

The crudity of the whore's approach and her blowsy appearance left a bitter taste in Jubal's mouth and he gulped at his whiskey, grateful for the fact that Nolan was tactful

* See – Jubal Cade: The Hungry Gun

enough not to press him on the point.

'Never could stand cheap tarts,' he said by way of explanation.

'Me neither,' agreed Nolan, 'if I want a woman I ride over to San Joaquin. They got a real nice house there.' He smiled appreciatively.

Jubal changed the subject by suggesting they set his quarters in order and, with Nolan leading the way, headed for the back of the tent.

Beyond the rear flap two rows of canvas formed a neatly spaced avenue, each tent erected with military precision. The first four on either side, Nolan explained, were occupied by his girls, the next two by himself and the barkeeps; the remaining four were used for storage purposes. He roused a sleepy-eyed man from his bed and set him to clearing out two tents. Jubal added some instructions of his own and returned to the saloon to wait.

Nolan organized the stabling of Jubal's horse and by late afternoon the tents were ready. A powerful smell of disinfectant wafted from the planking set down in the medical tent. A long wooden table stood to one side and a couple of canvas chairs to the other, a stove had been set up, its blackened smokestack protruding from a slash in the canvas ceiling, and a barrel of water had been placed outside. Jubal's own tent offered a cot, blankets and a washstand. The arrangements were simple in the extreme, but sufficient for Jubal's purposes. After all, he reminded himself, he had worked in worse surroundings.

Nolan had even organized a roughly-painted shingle with Jubal's name and the legend: *doctor*. Outside the saloon a more elaborate sign advertised the new service offered by the establishment.

Now Jubal had only to wait for patients.

They began coming in as night fell, grubby, work-worn men with the kind of injuries common to hard labour in makeshift surroundings. Jubal set two broken legs, lanced a boil, sutured numerous deep cuts and dressed and bandaged sundry minor wounds. By the time his last patient had limped back into the Golden Nugget Jubal was thirty dollars better off. His prices, he knew, were high by normal standards, but he was the only doctor in the territory and most of the miners were only too

26

glad to hand over gold or coins rather than miss precious digging time. Jubal banked his earnings with Nolan and ordered himself a whiskey.

He was leaning against the bar, slowly sipping the fiery liquid, when Nolan waved him over to a table and invited him to sit in on a poker session.

Jubal was more than ready to accept, although he had to take credit from Nolan for a hundred dollar stake. If his luck held, and he played with his usual skill, he could, he anticipated, come out ahead of the game.

The first few hands encouraged his optimism. Nolan was a skilful card player, but the other two men were miners first, gamblers a long second. They placed their bets and drew their cards with more faith in pure luck than card sense, and before long Jubal had payed off his debt to Nolan and still had forty dollars on the table in front of him. He was looking forward to increasing the pile when the game was interrupted.

The bat-wing doors of the saloon crashed open as a man walked heavily through them. Blood streaked his face from a gaping cut across his forehead, one arm hung uselessly by his side, the other clutched at a spreading red stain on his shirt front. He took three steps into the tent then toppled face down.

Jubal was on his feet and moving forward before the man hit the sand floor, eyeing the two arrows sticking out of his back.

'Get him into the tent!' It was an order and the whiplash in Jubal's voice stung the drinkers into action. Four men grabbed the body and carried it through the saloon as Jubal hurried before them.

Inside the tent, he administered morphine and began to cut the arrows free. From the man's pulse and the number of his wounds, Jubal knew there was little chance of saving his life, but his allegiance to his Hippocratic oath remained strong and he worked deftly to clean and bind the wounds.

The arrows left gaping holes in the man's back and when Jubal had finished removing the shafts, he knew that he could not attempt to remove the bullet that was lodged in the man's chest: he was too weak to stand the shock of operation. Instead, Jubal did what he could to cleanse the wound and make the miner as comfortable as possible. As he finished, Nolan shouldered his way through the crowd gathered outside the tent.

'That's Tam Gibbons,' he said when he saw the face, 'got a claim about five miles up river. Can he talk?'

'Yeah,' the voice was low and racked with pain at the effort, 'I kin talk.'

'Take it easy,' Jubal admonished, 'you're hurt pretty bad.'

'Doc,' grunted Gibbons, 'I'm dyin'. Thanks fer tryin', but we both know I'm finished.' He paused, spitting blood. 'Raiders hit the claim. Joe an' Billy are both dead. I got mounted an' rode out. That's how I stopped the arrows.' His voice had dropped to a low, slurred mutter. 'Fell off the damn' horse a mile back an' walked in.'

'Who were they?' Nolan urged.

'The same gang.' Anger strengthened Gibbons' voice. 'Apaches, Mexicans an' whites. Big guy with matched Colts and a scar rode in front.'

Jubal felt a sudden shock course through his body.

'A scar? Where?'

'Right across his forehead, groaned Gibbons, 'good-lookin' feller with a real evil grin. Like he enjoys killin'.'

'He does.' Jubal's voice was tight and throaty, hatred constricting his vocal cords. 'I know him.'

Cold anger stretched the skin taut across his cheekbones, so that the scar tissue over his nose showed white against his tan. In his mind he saw Lee Kincaid's face, laughing as he killed Mary, snarling like an animal as Jubal chased him into the mine shaft in Mexico.

His mind was working furiously. Kincaid must have escaped when the shaft fell in, got out through some escape tunnel; there couldn't be two men with a scar like that and a penchant for wanton slaughter. He turned to Nolan.

'Who's the law around here?'

'Ain't none,' replied Nolan carefully, 'except miners' law.'

He took command of the situation, speaking forcefully to the crowd outside.

'OK, let's move. Twenty men head for Tam's claim. They'll be gone by now, but you might pick up a trail. The rest stand ready to fight if we got to.'

Men were running for their horses when Nolan shouted again.

'Don't forget to bring the bodies in.'

It was almost an afterthought. It stopped Jubal, though, as he made for his own horse, reminding him of the dying man, tearing him between his duty as a doctor and his desire to find and kill Kincaid.

'Jubal,' it was as though Nolan sensed his torment, 'they'll be long gone by now. You ain't gonna find him out there. In fact it's more likely they'll hit the town. Either way, Tam needs you.'

'Yeah.' Jubal was angry with himself for permitting his emotions to govern his logic. 'You're right, Fred, I'll stay.'

He turned back to the miner, still conscious and still in pain, but determined to speak.

'Doc,' he whispered, 'I know you done what you could fer me an' I'm grateful. Don't have no money on me, so when I go I want you to have the claim. Nolan, you're witness to that.'

The saloon-keeper nodded.

Jubal looked thoughtful: a plan was forming in his mind that just might bring Mary's killer into his gunsights.

'Thanks, Tam,' he murmured as Gibbons coughed blood and died, 'you gave me an idea along with the mine.'

# CHAPTER FIVE

Jubal spent a long and sleepless night thinking about Lee Kincaid, but the following morning his determination overcame fatigue. He ate a hurried breakfast and rode out to his new-found claim. Nolan had told him where to find it, adding the pleasing information that Tam and his partners had always brought in a good amount of gold. That, whatever the outcome of Jubal's plan, should at least guarantee Andy Prescott's clinic fees for some time to come; and if all worked out as Jubal hoped, he would both kill Kincaid and end up richer.

The sun was high by the time he reached the mine and he was grateful for the cool shadows of the shaft. It was sunk horizontally into a high bank facing the Salt River, running a couple of hundred feet into the ground. At its farthest point, the shaft curved abruptly to the right, following the vein of glistening ore. The dead miners had already extended the tunnel along a fair part of the vein, so Jubal needed simply to hack the gold out, sluice it free of impurities and bring it in to the assay office. But before he began to work his inheritance, there were precautions he had to take.

Unloading the pack-animal he had brought with him, he hid its burden in several strategic places around the mine. Then he set to work.

That evening, tired and ravenously hungry, he returned to Nolan's saloon. He had placed fifty dollars' worth of nuggets in the bank and was ready to make more money tending injured miners. When he was finished he refused Nolan's invitation to play cards, choosing instead to collapse onto his cot for the night.

The next week passed in similar fashion. Jubal rode early to the claim, worked it all day and returned to doctor miners at dusk. Then he would play some poker before retiring early to bed. It was exhausting, but he was building up a healthy deposit in the bank and, more important to his plan, he was making sure that people heard about the rich vein he had struck. Sooner or later, he hoped, word would get back to the raiders and they would come looking for him.

They came halfway through the second week.

Jubal was washing gold in the sluice box when a bullet ploughed splinters over his shirt front. He grabbed the Spencer and powered himself across the sand to the entrance of the shaft.

Bullets spanged off the rock face, but the rough barricade he had built around the entrance protected him from direct fire. He waited, carefully extracting one of the bundles he had hidden near the entrance; then, casually, he lit a cheroot and waited for the frontal attack he knew would come soon.

Three Apaches headed the charge, screaming as they loped straight at his defence line. A cold grin twisted his compressed lips into a savage line as he sighted the rifle and fired three times. The first two shots knocked two Indians back on their heels, scarlet flowers exploding on their chests. The third doubled over as Jubal's bullet ripped through his lower belly, drenching his cotton leggings in blood. Incredibly, he kept moving with one hand holding in his entrails, the other an old Navy Colt. Pain made his firing erratic so that Jubal was able to aim with almost negligent ease, placing a shot clean between the hate-filled black eyes.

The Apache's head snapped back as the .30 calibre bullet tore away the back of his skull. His legs pumped him on even with the life blasted from his body and he hit the barricade like a human battering ram, bouncing off to sprawl in a spreading pool of crimson.

Jubal was uneasy as he pushed fresh cartridges into the Spencer. The attack had been suicidal, with no real chance of success, and he wondered if Kincaid — assuming it was the scarfaced man behind it — had planned it as a cover for something else.

His doubts were confirmed by a fusillade that echoed from two sides of the mine shaft, the ricochets forcing him to huddle in the dubious shelter of a pit prop. As he crouched, the firing ceased and a pair of highly-polished boots decorated with huge, silver Sonora spurs dropped into view from above. Before Jubal could bring his rifle to bear, he saw a concho-studded jacket and a swarthy, moustached face drop past the barricade.

The Mexican was taking a long chance, but he had swung

31

inside the cave mouth with his Colt blasting before Jubal could react. Shells lifted tatters of linen from his shirt sleeves as the Mexican fanned his gun and Jubal wondered if he had lost. Time seemed to slow as adrenalin pumped through his body and he remembered Bill McDonald's advice: anyone can fire fast; it's where the shots go that counts.

It seemed like a long time, although it could have been no more than a split second, before he brought up the Spencer and squeezed the trigger.

The Mexican screamed and flung his arms wide as the force of the bullet's impact catapulted him backwards over the barricade. His spurs caught in the woodwork as he fell, so that he hung upside down, sightless eyes surveying the battlefield with a blank stare as blood dripped steadily from the wound in his chest. Jubal left him where he hung; the corpse was an extra bulwark against the main attack.

Then fury consumed him like a newly-stoked furnace. Across the clearing in front of the mine he saw a tall figure, broad-shouldered and ruggedly handsome, a four-inch long scar spoiling the face. It was Kincaid.

Swiftly, as a dozen men raced towards him, Jubal raised the dynamite he had hidden, lighting the seconds-short fuse with the cheroot. The cord spluttered into life, trailing sparks as Jubal hurled the stick out over the barricade. Some of the attackers saw it coming and tried to dive for cover.

None made it.

The dynamite exploded in their midst with a shattering roar that lifted a cloud of smoke and sand, mingled with flying bodies, high into the afternoon air. Men screamed as their bones broke under the impact, tossing them like rag dolls in all directions. As the smoke cleared, Jubal saw a man with both legs pulped trying to drag himself to safety. He ignored the slow-moving target to fire at another, limping slowly towards the river. The bullet pushed the raider the few remaining feet to the water, smashing him face down into the Salt. He struggled madly, fighting against the spine broken by Jubal's shot, then drowned, unable to drag himself clear.

Jubal swung the rifle to cover the other attacker and ended his slow progress with a clean head shot.

Kincaid had disappeared from view and Jubal swore at his loss. He dared not go out looking for the man, even though every taut-strung nerve in his body prompted him to take that crazy chance. Instead, he remained pinned down in the tunnel, forced to await the next attack.

For a long time it was very quiet, the silence of the New Mexican day broken only by an occasional shot.

Then sudden thunder interrupted the quiet. The mine shaft was plunged abruptly into darkness, clouds of dust choking off Jubal's breath as the shattered remnants of his barricade fell around his ears. He wondered if the raiders had located one of his caches of dynamite and used it against him. He ran cautious hands over his body, but could find no sign of injury. Then an awful doubt hit him. The tunnel was dark, he could not see even his raised hand, held only inches from his face. Urgently, he rubbed at his eyes. They stung from the flying dust, watering as he massaged the sockets, but he remained in total darkness.

Groping blindly, he located the Spencer, cocking the rifle by instinct as he pulled back against the mine's wall. Then something burned his hand. He looked instinctively down and saw the faint glow of his cheroot, burning red in the blackness.

He was not blinded, so what, he wondered, had happened?

Warily, he probed the lightless tunnel, using the cheroot as a torch. Across the entrance rested a huge boulder, blocking it completely. Faint through the obstruction he heard a familiar voice.

'That's one stone he'll never roll away. If he gets out of that tomb, it'll be a miracle.'

# CHAPTER SIX

Jubal mouthed silent obscenities as he recognized the harsh voice of Lee Kincaid. He had never been quite so close to the man; nor blocked by so solid a barrier. Reluctantly, he accepted the fact that he was cut off from his quarry, trapped — he was forced to admit to himself — in a plugged mine. There was no way he could move the boulder that stoppered the shaft as effectively as a cork in a bottle; it sealed off the entrance like a great stone shutter that allowed through only a bare minimum of air. And that, after a while, began to turn stale.

By then, hoofbeats had told Jubal that the claim-jumpers had ridden off, taking with them, so far as he could gather, all the gold he had stashed outside the mine.

He swore again, and began to fumble through the pitch dark of the shaft. Almost reluctantly, he struck one of his few remaining matches, using the faint, red glow to rummage behind a pit-prop. He found the package he was looking for, and carefully, holding the spluttering match in his teeth, laid the dynamite down against the boulder. He uttered silent thanks that he had thought to cache the explosive in and around the mine. Then, working solely with his surgeon's deft fingers, he readied the fuse for ignition. When he was finished he risked striking another match. The dynamite was set firmly beneath the rock, the short fuse extended inwards to the shaft.

Jubal refused to allow himself time to think about the consequences. Instead, he lit the fuse and powered himself backwards in a long dive that brought him far back, rolling behind the tenuous shelter of a mine prop.

As he landed the dynamite blew.

A great, gusting roar of solid, hot power filled the shaft. Dust roiled around him as a wave of naked, raw force picked him up in the air and hurled him farther back down the mine. Thunder filled his ears as jagged splinters of broken stone and shattered wood rained down on his body, ripping through cloth and flesh in a funnelling torrent of destruction.

Deafened, blinded by the dust and smoke, aching through-

34

out his whole body, Jubal staggered to his feet. Half-unconscious he tottered forward through the smoking turmoil, dust-filled eyes endeavouring to see through the black mist flooding the mine.

Faintly, like some dim promise of a hopeful future, he spotted a glimmer of light ahead of him. Blindly he walked forward, and as he walked the glimmer grew brighter, spreading, magnifying, promising.

It seemed like an eternity, but at last he reached it, just as his lungs felt like they were choking on the near-solid miasma of the explosion.

Coughing, his eyes streaming unfelt tears, he staggered into daylight over the blasted remnants of the sealing rock. Blinking the muck from his eyes, he surveyed the entrance. Bodies littered the area in front of the mine, stretched in their own blood beneath the pall of grey smoke that billowed and lifted lazily in the hot air. Jubal ignored them as he walked slowly towards the river, picking his way so that he did not fall as he forced his weakened legs to carry him over the yards to the water's edge.

Once there he fell gratefully forward onto hands and knees, dipping his head into the cool, clear stream, allowing the Salt River to wash away the effects of his escape.

He stayed by the riverbank for a long time, waiting for his head to clear and the muck to drain from his eyes. Then he stood up and headed for the pinto pony, restlessly stamping off to one side of the mine.

Wearily he hauled himself onto the pony's back, wincing at the pain that shot through his body as the animal began to move, but forcing himself to ignore it as he allowed the pinto to pick its own path back to the mining camp.

The explosion, confined within the narrow space of the shaft, had blasted shockwaves against Jubal that could easily have killed a weaker man. It was only his determination to survive and kill Kincaid that held him in the saddle, and as it was, blood dribbled freely from his nostrils and ears, smearing the pony's mane with a sticky, dark brown mess as he hung low over its neck. The water had gone some way to clearing his senses, but he remained, at best, only semi-conscious.

Sheer will-power held Jubal in the saddle as the nervous horse walked wearily into the camp, its rider looking more like a corpse than the grinning young man who had ridden out that morning.

The first person to spot him was the whore called Frankie.

'Doc!' she shouted as she ran across the street, throwing long shadows out of the setting sun, 'you're all bloody.'

'Shame, isn't it?' Jubal managed a weak smile. 'I thought no-one would notice.'

Then he fell off the horse.

He came to fast and painfully, his eyes opening to a blaze of sunlight that drove needlepoint tattoos like drumbeats through his skull. Groaning, he closed his eyes, allowing the red haze that shone from the inner lids to wash over his mind, taking it back towards oblivion. Within the confines of his cranium, his brain seemed to be pounding itself against the bone walls of his head; and it was difficult to tell exactly where the aches in his body began and ended.

He moved his lips with considerable effort. 'Let me be.'

Down the long, lonely corridors of pain he recognized a voice.

'Reckon he'll live.' It was Nolan. 'By rights he shouldn't, but I think this one will.'

Jubal stopped listening and drifted away on the welcoming, warming, embracing sea of unconsciousness.

When he next awoke he found that he could open his eyes without pain flooding his mind. It was dark outside and the only light came from a dimmed kerosene lantern set behind his cot. Nolan sat on a chair close to his bed, the gambler's grey eyes full of concern. When Jubal tried to sit up Nolan pushed him back onto the cot with hands that were surprisingly strong, but none the less gentle.

'Take it easy, Jubal,' he murmured, 'you came close to dying there, so don't push it now.'

Jubal lay back, assessing the damage to his body.

'How long was I out?'

'You rode in Tuesday,' said Nolan, 'it's Saturday night now.' He paused to sip the whiskey he held. 'We figgered you for a goner.'

Jubal forced a grin that threatened to crack his face.

'I got too much to do.'

Nolan shook his head. 'I saw a couple of men a while back,

36

tried to blow a seam loose. The stick went off before they got outta the shaft. One lost both legs, the other's blind an' deaf. He was closest to the entrance.'

He took a long swig of whiskey.

'Jubal, you are one hell of a lucky guy.'

Jubal took advantage of Nolan's contemplation to sit up and reach for the whiskey.

'A purpose in life gives a man a lot to live for,' he said with mock seriousness, disengaging the whiskey glass from Nolan's hand.

He coughed as he swallowed the fierce liquor, feeling it spread fire through his belly, easing the aches that still assailed him.

'I thought you weren't supposed to drink when you got stomach injuries,' protested Nolan.

'Dammit, Fred,' Jubal grinned, feeling better already, 'who's the doctor around here?'

He returned the empty glass, which Nolan promptly filled, and began – cautiously – to explore his body.

'Anyway, what injuries do I have?'

'Well,' Nolan said slowly, 'like you say, you're the doc, but as far as I could tell you got a couple of busted ribs, enough cuts to make you up like a slab of pork an' bruises to cover the lot.'

Jubal, feeling better now, pushed back the blankets and began a thorough examination of his injuries. Although relatively minor, they were extensive, running from the cuts on his face down to the swelling purple bruises that decorated his torso, abdomen and legs. His trained fingers told him that three ribs were broken, though not seriously enough to cause internal damage, and numerous muscles twisted sufficiently to slow him down for several days. Mentally, he diagnosed his own case and prescribed rest and medicine; he wondered as he did so whether or not he would stick to his own regime.

Probably not, he thought, with Kincaid loose in the territory. Still, he would rest up for a while: when he finally hunted down Mary's scarfaced murderer he knew he would have to be in peak condition to kill the man.

'Tell you what, Fred,' he grinned, his customary good-humoured look returning to his face, 'you keep me supplied with food and whiskey and I'll promise to lay up for a few days.'

'Food an' whiskey, hey?' Nolan matched Jubal's smile. 'But you ain't working. At those rates, who needs a doctor in the house?'

# CHAPTER SEVEN

Jubal bandaged his broken ribs afresh as soon as Nolan had gone, wrapping the white linen tight around the blue and purple bumps where the bones pushed against his midriff. He groped for his medical valise and found it close to the cot; from it he took a small ampule of morphine and a hypodermic syringe. With no hot water available, he cleansed the hypodermic in the whiskey Nolan had left him and injected the drug into his left forearm.

He knew that morphine killed pain and, judiciously, had used it on patients before, when circumstances warranted a serious pain-killer. But he had always been wary of the stuff: he had seen men and women in London, during his time as a medical student, who had been given too much. Mindless, slavering slaves to the drug that was supposed to save their lives, they had made Jubal cautious of using it. Now, though, he felt prepared to take the risk, balancing his need to recuperate quickly against the possibility of addiction.

Soon, with a soothing gentleness, sleep washed over him. He was long gone when Frankie entered the tent with a tray of food.

'Hell,' muttered the whore, 'he don't buy me, he don't pay me an' now he don't even want to eat with me.'

She set the tray beside the cot, smiled in spite of herself as she looked down at the burned, marked face reposing in sleep like a child's, and arranged the blankets around Jubal's form. Penetrate the armour this man threw up around himself, she thought almost tenderly, and there was one hell of a good human being underneath, the kind a woman could love. She looked at the boyish face, broken teeth exposed as he slept, and felt a sudden wash of motherly tenderness come over her. Maybe, if she'd met a man like this – how many years ago? – she would have a different role now. Wife, mother? Who could tell?

Frankie shrugged her heavily powdered shoulders, hitching the tatty red dress up over her swelling breasts, and left the tent. It was no good thinking of maybes: she had a trade and there were too many eager gold-grubbers waiting, to waste time on one wounded medical man who hadn't even given her a second glance.

She was thinking about it as she walked back to her waiting clients. Frankie, whose real name was Mary O'Reilley, had been born to poor farmers in Nebraska. She had been exactly twelve years old when a cousin, drunk on the crude corn liquor her father had supplied to celebrate her birthday, had raped her behind the chicken sheds of the family farm. When he refused to marry her, her father had shot him dead. Two weeks later Paw had his guts spilled at close range by a scattergun and Mary and her mother had taken to the road, with nothing more than their bodies to pay the way. For a while they had done well. Maw hadn't been more than thirty years old and they made the kind of double act that appealed mightily to ageing businessmen in every town from Lincoln to Tallahassee.

Business had slowed when Maw caught the whore's occupational hazard and died as a result, but Mary – now known as Frankie, counterpart to her mother, Jonie – had kept on moving. There hadn't really been much else to do. Topeka, St. Louis, Atchison, Dodge; she'd seen them all, the smug bankers and the sweaty cowboys, the gamblers and the gunmen. Under the sheets they were mostly the same.

The cowtowns had lead to the railcamps, those to the mining settlements. Where a dollar was to be made any man with the money to pay could find Mary O'Reilley, ready, blowsy and willing to oblige.

She was still thinking about her career when a .44 calibre bullet ended everything.

The chunk of lead ricochetted off a tent pole so that it was flattened out and twice as large as normal when it hit her directly between her sagging breasts. Half-spent as the bullet was, it still smashed through her breast-bone in a spinning, ripping flight that hurtled her back towards Jubal's tent as she sprayed blood over the red lantern advertising her own sleeping place.

Mary O'Reilley gave up her dreams along with her life as she tumbled on her back, for once without a man on top of her, spat out what little was left of her blasted lungs, and died.

Over her black garters, obscenely displayed in the rictus of death, bullets sprayed, ripping through canvas and flesh to decimate whores and clients alike, locking them together in death's long eternity, each flesh-blasting shell guaranteeing a longer tryst than either prostitute or miner had anticipated.

Inside the saloon tent men tumbled dead, spitting beer and blood over their cards, screaming and dying in the very moments of their pleasure as the lead storm ripped through the Golden Nugget.

Jubal slept through it all.

It probably saved his life, for had he seen the man who led the attackers he would have risked the bullets that raked the street in his attempt to reach Kincaid. The scarfaced man rode at the head of his renegade band, leading them in a wild charge through the tent town, firing at random into tents and shacks. The few people too slow in getting off the street were either ridden down or shot to death. The sporadic fire of the defenders did nothing to deter the raiders. Two men were blown from their horses, tumbling heavily onto the sand where bullets beat them down into silence, but the rest thundered on, ignoring their wounded and dead.

The whole thing took no longer than a few minutes, Kincaid laughing as he galloped away into the Sierra Mogallon, leaving behind a litter of corpses.

Mary O'Reilley was dead, and with her ten other men and women. Fifteen men, wounded in varying degrees, made their way to the Golden Nugget.

Three died before Nolan could bring Jubal out of his drug-induced sleep to examine them.

Once awake, however, Jubal went to work. His ribs hurt abominably and he still felt groggy, but he forced himself to concentrate on his new-found patients, drawing bullets and binding wounds with a cool professionalism that belied the seething anger inside his calm exterior.

Black coffee kept him going as the rising sun lanced shafts of light over the bloodied, battered township. Jubal kept working until close on midday, when he despatched the last of the wounded to the makeshift hospital tent. As the man, heavily bandaged where an arrow had penetrated his rib-cage, was carried out, Nolan appeared with a large shot-glass full of whiskey.

'Private reserve,' he grinned, handing the drink to Jubal, 'I keep it for special occasions. Right now, you look like a special occasion.'

'Thanks,' murmured Jubal, 'I can use it.'

He was dog tired and the broken ribs hurt him, his need for sleep was fighting hard with the desire to climb on a horse and go looking for Kincaid, but he knew that caution and planning were the better part of valour in this case; so he sipped the whiskey and waited for Nolan to speak.

He did not have to wait long.

'I've been talkin' with the boys,' said the saloon owner. 'We figger that raid was for what you did to them out at the mine. They ain't never been hurt that bad before an' we reckon you got them riled up.'

He sipped his own drink as he watched Jubal's drawn face, dark shadows standing out under his eyes in which showed a cold anger.

'Seems like you know more about that scarfaced guy than anyone else. Leastways, you come closer to him than anyone else who ever came back alive.'

'Not close enough,' Jubal's voice was bitter.

'But you know things about him,' continued Nolan, 'better'n us. You got more idea of the way he thinks, what he's like to do.' He broke off as Jubal nodded.

'Yeah.' Memories of pain and sudden loss filled Jubal's eyes. 'I know him some.'

'That's why we reckoned you'd be the man for the job.'

'What job?' Jubal became abruptly aware that Nolan had lined him up for some task other than doctoring. Whether or not he woul·' accept it was a decision he would take when he heard the terms. His sole purpose right now was to find Kincaid and kill the man.

'Well,' Nolan was for once at a loss for words as Jubal's deep-set brown eyes probed coldly into his. 'We were talking about formin' a militia. You know, a protective association. There ain't no law up here an' the Army ain't about to come in, so we figgered on forming our own guard force an' gettin' a posse headed up into the Mogallons to find them raiders.'

He broke off to pour two more whiskeys.

'An' we want you to lead it.'

Jubal stayed silent as he ran over the implications in his

mind. Now that he knew for sure that Kincaid led the raiders, he was staying in the Salt River camp until one of them was dead. His original plan had been to draw the raiders to him in the hope of killing the scarfaced man; that hope had gone for the moment; but maybe an organized hunt? The thought was tantalizing.

'Let's go talk about it.'

As he spoke, Jubal was pulling on his jacket, adjusting the loosened black tie around his collar. He set the grey derby on his close-cropped black hair and followed Nolan out of the saloon tent.

A short way down the rough boardwalk, they came to the big tent that was used for public meetings. Inside, most of the camp's population stood waiting, boot-heels nervously drumming the packed sand that was the only floor.

Nolan walked Jubal through the crowd to the wooden platform at the far end. The crowd grew silent as they mounted the roughly planed wood; then, like the slow surge of a big wave coming in to break, applause filled the tent.

Nolan smiled at Jubal.

'You made quite a reputation here, doc. You know that?'

Jubal shook his head and waited for the noise to die down.

For the better part of two hours he listened to the miners. The Salt River claims were rich, but the men who did the work were robbed blind by the renegades; lately the raids had gotten worse; they needed a militia to protect their mines; that meant they needed someone to organize the force; the doc had proved his worth, both medically and with a gun, and he knew the leader of the renegades. Would he command the militia?

Jubal was more accustomed to acting alone; since Mary's death he had been alone except for Andy. But the idea of controlling an organized force dedicated to hunting out Kincaid promised him the fulfilment of his desires.

He accepted.

Nolan had already organized terms: Jubal, as commander of the Miners' Volunteer Militia was to receive 1% of all the town's takings each week. In return, he would administer free medicine and lead the militia in its campaign against the raiders. It was a profitable enterprise and Jubal accepted readily: now he could easily guarantee Andy's clinic fees.

'In the morning,' he announced to his newly organized troops, 'I want twenty men, armed and ready to ride. We'll go looking for Kincaid.'

He avoided the ensuing celebrations in favour of a night's sleep.

Come sunrise, Jubal was refreshed and ready to go. It took him another hour to gather his posse, picking the men with Nolan's help, selecting, as far as possible, unmarried miners. His chief criterion, however, was the ability to use a gun and of the twenty volunteers, he had faith in only about three. The rest were simply eager to go along and would provide little more than erratic firepower.

As they rode out, Jubal wondered if it would not have been better to go after the raiders on his own.

At the head of the band a half-breed Navajo called Smokey Joe was venting his tribe's hereditary hatred of the Apaches by picking the trail. From Jubal's claim he followed the outlaws' track through the desolation of the Mogallons. Jubal had learned a little of the trackers' art when he had lived with the Cheyenne, but the turned stones and broken grass blades that marked the path for Smokey Joe remained virtually invisible to his eyes.

He was grateful to have the half-breed along: he saved the posse time. And time, Jubal was sure, was the key to their problem. Somewhere in the mountains, the renegades had a camp to which they returned after their raids. It was unlikely that they would expect any pursuit so soon after the attack, and that might – just – give the militia the advantage of surprise.

They made good time while the light lasted, then made camp as dusk fell. Jubal vetoed the idea of fires, to the disgust of his companions, and insisted on a cold camp. Grumbling bitterly as the cold of the sierra shut down for the night, the posse chewed on dry meat, washed down with water from the canteens, before settling down to sleep. Jubal posted four guards, taking the second shift himself, and wondered how long it would take them to catch up with Kincaid and his men.

He found out the next day.

Smokey Joe was picking his way across a plateau dotted with low-lying scrub, his keen black eyes coursing back and forth over the ground, when Kincaid's presence made itself felt.

The half-breed grunted deep in his throat, reaching up to pluck at the arrow sprouting suddenly from his windpipe. His fingers were closing around the painted shaft when two more missiles hit his chest. With a strangled groan, he slid sideways off his horse, crashing face down on the ground so that all three arrows were pushed up through his body like bloody pins stuck through a rag doll.

As he fell, Jubal kicked his pinto forward, raising the Spencer as the animal hit full stride. He was unsure of the enemy's numbers and had only a vague idea of their position. But rather than risk being surrounded, he preferred to carry the attack to the ambushers. He galloped through the scrub, firing the rifle as he went.

One shot, at least, found a target, for an Apache erupted from the bushes in front of him, clutching at a bleeding shoulder as he tried to run from the path of Jubal's headlong charge. He never made it. Instead, the big-chested pinto hit him full in the back, pitching him over onto his chest as the pony's hooves hammered over his spine. The Indian screamed once as his backbone snapped, then fell silent as the horsemen following Jubal rode his corpse into the ground.

There was no more sound and no more movement except the restless stamping of the posse's horses and the angry muttering of the men. Whoever had been with the Apache was gone, disappearing as though the scrubland had never hidden ambushers.

Jubal cursed at the loss of Smokey Joe and called the posse into a semblance of order. No-one else could follow the trail as well, so Jubal was forced to take the task on himself.

Now, though, he rode with two men, rifles to hand, close on either side.

Two hours later one of them died.

Once again the attack was silent, arrows thudding into the miner's body, this time from behind. Two feathered his ribs and two more hit him as he pitched from the saddle. He was dead before he hit the sand and the posse was thrown into total confusion. In spite of Jubal's orders, the men scattered to either side of the trail, each one seeking the hidden attackers.

Three more died in that way, arrows whistling out of the

45

sun-baked morning to snuff life from protesting bodies. Then it was quiet again. The ambushers were gone as though they had never been there.

For the remainder of the day things were quiet, the posse pushing on through the scrub at an easy, wary canter, rifles cocked and ready for another attack. None came, and they made camp at nightfall, posting double guards.

In the morning eight more men were dead, knifed in the night.

It was the breaking point for the miners. They were ready enough to go up against the raiders in open fighting, that they could understand. But this ambuscading threw them; the thought of a silent arrow or a knife cutting off their lives shook them. As they gathered in the corpses, stripped of clothing and hair, they reached a decision: the Miners' Volunteer Militia was finished, all they wanted to do was get back to town alive.

Seven didn't. Arrows picked them from their mounts as they rode desperately for the tenuous safety of the township.

Jubal was the only survivor. Gaunt-faced and bitterly weary, he rode slowly back into the tent town, ignoring the curious stares of the passers-by as he headed for Nolan's saloon.

He dismounted and walked in, carrying the Spencer. At the bar he called for a bottle of whiskey, conscious of the eyes probing his back, the taste of defeat bitter in his mouth. Nolan joined him there, silent and for once unsmiling . . .

'Don't say anything,' Jubal muttered, bitter bile in his mouth, 'we lost out. Twenty to one, with me the one.'

Nolan sipped his drink and maintained a judicious quiet.

'Dammit, Fred,' Jubal continued, 'I took those men up there to find Kincaid. He found us, instead. And now there's twenty men dead, thanks to me.'

He paused to swallow a shot of whiskey, and Nolan took advantage of the silence that had shut down like a winter night over the saloon.

'Hell, Jubal,' he forced a cheerful note into his voice, 'you couldn't help it. We all knew what we were goin' up against.'

'Yeah.' Jubal's voice was low and harsh. 'And I took twenty men up against it. Just to die.'

Nolan fell silent at the raw anger in Jubal's voice, watching the compressed lips and taut-drawn skin across the other man's cheekbones. Somehow the blazing eyes and flared nostrils of the man in the dust-stained grey suit closed his mouth tighter than a fist.

'Just to die.' Jubal went on, finishing the whiskey and picking up the Spencer. 'Next time I'll operate on my own.' He picked up the medical bag in his left hand. 'Cancer needs cutting out. And only one surgeon can do that.'

He hefted the rifle as he spoke, and walked away.

'You're the doctor,' Nolan muttered as he watched Jubal move towards the rear of the saloon.

# CHAPTER EIGHT

Jubal rode out at sun-up, hunched down under the stormcoat against the dawn chill, his medical valise strapped to the saddle and the Spencer sheathed close to his right hand. Deliberately, he had started out before the Salt River camp awoke; he wanted to move alone, partly to pay off old debts, partly because he felt the need to atone for the twenty more recent deaths.

Either way, he figured to hunt Kincaid and his band alone.

He followed the trail out to his claim and from there up into the Sierra Mogallon, taking the same route the posse had ridden three days earlier.

Along the way he saw the sepulchral signs of that earlier venture: the bones were white by now, picked clean by the vultures and the ants. They bleached in the sun, where they had fallen with no time for the short-lived militia to bring them in for burial. As he rode by, Jubal cursed Kincaid, although he never allowed his anger to interfere with his careful scanning of the terrain.

This time, though, there were no waiting ambushers, so that his first camp was relatively comfortable, despite the fireless night.

He kept on the same way for five more days, basing his direction on trailing skill, guesswork and blind luck. He knew the renegades had to have their camp somewhere in the Mogallons and reckoned on quartering the ground until he found it; or they found him. Either way, he did not care too much. The driving force at that moment was the urgent need to confront Kincaid, taking whatever chances came his way.

Wary though he was, the first chance took Jubal by surprise.

A lariat settled around his shoulders as he pushed the pinto through the rocks. It yanked him bodily from his saddle, smashing wind from his lungs as he hit the ground. Before he could draw the Colt from its shoulder holster, a second rope landed neatly over his wrists, binding them firmly together. A third pulled his feet from under him as he tried to rise. Spitting sand out of his mouth, Jubal heard a guttural voice speaking heavily accented English.

'I am Natchez. We shall talk.'

The speaker was tall for an Apache, six feet or more, with raven-black hair flowing over wide shoulders. Deep-set black eyes studied Jubal impassively from a broad, brown face that looked no more than twenty years old. The lever-action Winchester pointing at Jubal's midriff was a good deal younger; there was a name picked out on the stock: Tom. One of the dead miners had been named Tom.

There wasn't very much Jubal could say, so he kept his mouth shut.

Natchez grunted something in his own language and a second brave stepped around from behind Jubal to loose the rope binding his feet. The others stayed around his wrists and arms as Natchez lifted the converted Colt from its holster under Jubal's jacket.

'Get up,' he ordered.

It was difficult without the use of his arms, but Jubal struggled to his feet, looking up at the tall Indian.

The brave studied him with interest.

'You follow a long time,' he remarked in what was almost a conversational tone, 'the others all die, but you keep on coming. Why? You not fear death?'

'I'm looking for a man,' Jubal said tightly, 'my quarrel's with him, not you.'

'Bad place to look for men.' Amusement sounded in the Apache's voice. 'You find me instead.'

Jubal knew the brave was playing a game with him, a deadly game that could easily end in his death, but so long as the man kept talking, he had a slender chance of staying alive. It was almost, he thought, like a poker session, only words were the cards and his life the stake.

He decided to draw afresh.

'A scarfaced man called Lee Kincaid. He killed my wife. I aim to kill him.'

Natchez grunted and showed his hand.

'Kincaid enjoys killing. Maybe he kill you. We go see.'

Jubal sighed inwardly: the gambit had worked, the cards were down and another round about to begin.

He stumbled as an Apache pushed him towards his horse,

49

then stood silent as the lariat was removed from his shoulders. His wrists were left tied and he climbed awkwardly into the saddle. Around him, the Indians mounted their own wiry ponies and, with Natchez in the lead, began to canter through the scrub. One brave retained the rope binding Jubal's hands, so that he was forced to clutch the pommel of his saddle as he was dragged onward, concentrating on staying in the precarious seat as the Indians, oblivious or uncaring, led him on at their own speed.

It was a hard ride, with Natchez pushing a fast pace until they reached a wall of rock standing up from the plateau like the battlements of some ancient fortification. They slowed as they approached the rocks and Jubal had a chance to study the terrain. The sandstone buttress was a natural fort with lookouts posted along the rim, watching the open ground stretching out in front. They recognized the party riding in and waved rifles in greeting. Natchez headed the group straight at the rock, taking them through a narrow defile that opened onto a wider trail, so that Apaches rode on either side of Jubal as he came into a rock-rimmed bowl, set like a deep saucer within the surrounding cliffs.

A spring bubbled in the centre of the bowl and around its clear waters stood the hogans of Natchez' people. To one side of the Indian village there was a cluster of canvas tents and throughout the grassy area Indians and white men sprawled, watching the group coming in.

They reined up near a corral of piñon branches, Jubal's captor jerking the lariat so that Jubal was hauled abruptly out of his saddle. For the second time that day, he hit the ground, groaning with pain as his damaged ribs protested the shock.

Then he forgot his hurts as he spotted the man walking towards them.

Tall and nearly handsome, his rugged good looks were spoiled by the stark white scar running across his forehead. Jubal climbed to his feet as he recognized Kincaid, the sight of his quarry stretching his mouth to a thin, tight line as raw hate blazed in his eyes.

Natchez spotted the fury-ridden mask of his captive's face and looked over at the other white man.

'Kincaid.' It was a blunt statement. 'You found your man.'

'Yeah,' grunted Jubal. 'Now I got to get him.'

Natchez laughed. 'You talk big for a man with his hands tied.'

'Let me loose, then,' snarled Jubal, watching Kincaid come closer, 'and I'll show you some action.'

Hate negated his logic as he struggled blindly against the rope holding his wrists together. He was oblivious of the watching Apaches or the whites clustered around Kincaid: at that moment in time all that occupied his mind was the thought of getting free and attacking the grinning killer.

Kincaid's boot brought him savagely back to reality. Without pausing in his long-legged stride, the outlaw swung his foot up hard into Jubal's groin. The smaller man doubled over as pain flooded through his body. He fell to his knees, clutching the core of his agony as tears misted his eyes and nausea rose in his throat. For long, pain-racked moments, he rolled on the grass in a foetal position, trying to quell the bile filling his stomach. It was a losing game and he rolled face down as vomit spewed from his mouth. He waited until the spasm had passed, the waves of agony slowly receding until he could hear Kincaid's voice.

He was arguing with Natchez, urging the young Indian to kill Jubal immediately. Natchez, however, was in favour of waiting; it appeared that his father, the tribe's chief, was away from camp, and his son was chary of killing the captive out of hand, preferring to await his father's return.

Slowly, as he regained control, Jubal became aware of the tension pervading the camp. Grouped around and behind him, stood the Apaches; facing them, Kincaid's men fingered their weapons. It seemed that little love was lost between the two groups, their murderous working relationship was an uneasy alliance rather than a genuine partnership. Jubal tried to make capital of the tension.

'What's up, Kincaid,' he shouted, 'you can't get your own way?'

Kincaid snarled an unintelligible reply and Natchez gestured to one of his men.

Something heavy crashed against Jubal's head and he pitched forward into a big black pit. He came to cold and hungry, his ribs were hurting again and a bitter taste filled his mouth. His hands were tied to his ankles, so that his body was curved back on itself in a bow shape. He felt rotten, but he was, he reminded himself, alive. That, at least, was something.

He lay there in darkness for a long time, listening to the sounds outside. He was in a hogan, the floor bare soil, the curving walls faintly visible as his eyes grew accustomed to the darkness. It was night and a cloth of some kind covered the entrance to the hut, thin enough to permit a little of the fireglow from outside to filter through. Sufficient, at least, for Jubal to realize that the hogan was undecorated, unlived in, and that an armed guard stood by the entrance. Not, he thought ruefully, that there was much point in posting a guard. After struggling for several minutes, he had realized that there was no chance of escaping his bonds: the rawhide thongs held him as firmly as chains. All he could do was make himself as comfortable as possible and wait upon events.

He could not see the watch in his vest pocket, but he thought about two hours had passed before the entrance flap was pulled aside and three men came in.

Natchez was one, carrying a torch that threw flickering light over the interior of the hogan. Kincaid was another, but it was the third man who caught Jubal's attention.

Gnarled like some ancient tree so that it was impossible to guess his age, he was bent over beneath a hunched back that pushed his head forward over his chest, bare in the torchlight and criss-crossed with old scars. Bright black eyes studied Jubal carefully, but the prisoner didn't see them. He was staring at the Apache's left arm. Where his hand should have been there was a gleaming metal hook. The wickedly pointed curve was lashed to the Indian's wrist with rawhide thongs that looked as though they were grown into the flesh itself.

The man split his lips in what might have been a smile on another face.

'Men call me Claw,' he said in good English, 'I have to decide if you will die.'

# CHAPTER NINE

Jubal forced himself to take his eyes away from the weird appendage and look back at the Indian's face. Claw seemed totally unconscious of the effect he produced, as though he had lived long enough with his twisted body to accept it as normal and expected other people to do the same.

'Kincaid says we should kill you now.' His voice was a throaty rasp that carried more expression than most Indians'. 'My son says you deserve a chance.'

His eyes gleamed with malicious amusement as he reached out to prod Jubal with the hook.

'What do you say?'

'Let me fight Kincaid.' It was as much a plea as an answer. 'I came a long way to kill him. Give me the chance now.'

Claw was genuinely pleased with Jubal's answer, nodding his head sagely in appreciation.

'You speak well for a white man,' he murmured. 'Most squeal for mercy when we take them. And then die screaming when we kill them.' He chuckled in remembered appreciation. 'But no, Kincaid is too valuable.'

'Hell, Claw,' Kincaid interrupted, 'I can take the little runt anytime. Let him fight me.'

Claw's glance shoved the words back down the white man's throat. It was cold and angry and it stopped Kincaid like a blow.

'No,' the chief continued, 'he can get us guns, which we need to fight the *pinda-lick-oye* who steal our land. You will not fight him.'

He paused, thinking for a moment.

'I have heard the words of my son, Natchez. He tells me you fight like an Indian, so you will be granted the trial of an Indian. You will face the run of the arrow. Untie him.' He gestured to Natchez as he turned to leave.

The young brave unsheathed a knife and cut Jubal free. As he rose, the prisoner spoke.

'What,' he asked, 'is the run of the arrow?'

'A trial,' said Natchez, 'of a man's strength.'

He broke off to stare hard at Jubal as he spoke, as though gauging the power in the white man's body.

'An arrow is fired,' he continued, 'and you must run to it. That distance is free ground, beyond it you become as the rabbit when the dogs are hunting. Our dogs are the fleetest runners in the tribe, and you must escape them to live. When you reach the arrow they will come after you. I shall be one of them.'

Jubal grinned ruefully.

'What about weapons?' He asked. 'Do I get to carry any?'

'A knife only,' Natchez replied, something that looked almost like sympathy showing in his dark eyes. 'Rest now. In the morning you will need all your strength.'

'Thanks for the advice,' Jubal muttered cynically as the young Apache left the hogan, 'it's good to know someone cares.'

Natchez caught the last words and turned in the entrance, a wolfish smile showing his even teeth.

'I care about the hunt,' he said. 'An easy kill is boring.'

'I'll do my best to give you value for money,' answered Jubal as the cloth flap closed out the light.

He settled himself down and tried to sleep. The floor of the hogan was hard and cold, the cracked clay walls letting in the night chill of the high sierras, but he had learned to live with discomfort since coming west. And, further, the man who had bequeathed him the Spencer rifle had once written him about a trick he used during the Civil War campaigns. Long dead now, the man's advice might still serve to save Jubal's life as his gun had done on many occasions.

Jubal stretched out on his back, his legs straight, arms at his side. Concentrating hard, he willed all feeling from his feet, forcing his aching muscles to relax. Gradually, he extended the concentration upwards through his entire body, breathing slowly as he felt his body go limp. Soon he felt as though he was melding with the ground itself, an easy, reassuring calm flowing over him. He slept.

He was awakened by the sharp pain in his side. When he opened his eyes he saw that it came from the foot of an Apache nudging him in the ribs.

He sat up, pushing the brave's foot away as he did so. The

Indian grinned and beckoned Jubal to follow him, standing aside as he rose to his feet and headed for the entrance. Outside, bright sunlight made him blink as he scanned the village. Although the sun was barely over the rim of the protecting cliffs, the *rancheria* was up and active. Cooking pots sizzled over open fires, tended by blank-faced women; grubby, grinning children gathered to watch the new prisoner, shouting insults, recognizable even though in Apache, as he made his way through the clustered huts.

In the centre of the camp, his guard motioned for him to stop, leaving him under the watchful gaze of two other Indians as he walked over to Claw, crouched close to a blazing fire with Natchez at his side.

The chief's son was sweating visibly as he sat beside his father. Jubal shivered in the dawn cold, noticing that Claw was wrapped in a heavy red blanket. And something else, something that the flickering torchlight of the previous interview had concealed. The front of the blanket was a darker red, a stained, caking brown colour: Claw was badly wounded.

In the daylight, Jubal could see it in the man's face. What he had taken for age the night before was the harsh marking of pain. The hunched back was still there, legacy of some old fight, but the pushed-forward head and stooped gait was not entirely due to that deformity, rather it was the belly-clutching defence against internal agony that a man assumes when gutshot.

Suddenly, Jubal saw a chance.

He waited until the two Apaches pushed him towards the chief and then he spoke.

'Claw.' He ignored the blow that landed hard on his back. 'You are hurt.'

The second blow knocked him down onto his knees, but he went on talking.

'You are hurt, but I can help you.'

A kick sprawled him face-down in the grass as a moccasin landed on his neck, pressing his mouth against the turf. Then it lifted and he raised his head to look at Claw.

'It does not need a white man to tell me that,' grunted the Apache, though a faint hint of interest showed in his face. 'But why should it concern you?'

'Because I'm a doctor.' Jubal said it fast, before anyone

55

could shut him up more permanently. 'A shaman, healer.' He struggled for the Spanish word, remembering that was the Apaches' second language. '*Un médico.*'

'I speak English,' said Claw, and Jubal could discern pain in his voice, 'better than you speak Spanish.'

He paused to cough, trailing long strands of bloody spittle over the stained blanket. Jubal took swift advantage of the pause.

'I'm a *doctor*.' he emphasised the word. 'I can help you.'

Claw gestured to the guards, motioning them away from Jubal's prone figure. Then he waited until Jubal stood up, raising a tired hand to indicate that his prisoner should speak.

'I can see,' said Jubal urgently, 'that you are hurt. Maybe I can help you.'

'How?' grunted Claw, his remaining hand crabbing unconsciously at his stomach. 'The shaman of my people has tended me through all the hours of the darkness, yet still the pain burns in my belly. What can one white-eyes do? One small man brought in like a trussed chicken to be butchered; what can he do?'

Jubal ignored both the insult and the threat. In the row of seated figures behind Claw he could see Kincaid, smiling like a lobo wolf facing a sick sheep, and within him he felt the burning need to kill the man. Nothing else mattered, so long as he could achieve that ultimate, deadly goal.

'On my horse,' he said carefully, 'there is ... was,' he corrected, 'a black bag. It contains white magic. The magic I learned across the wide sea, in the country where I studied the white man's art of healing.'

'The English land?' Claw asked, amusement showing around the pain in his face.

Jubal was taken aback. He knew that the American Indians were not foolish, but he had hardly anticipated an Apache chief understanding intercontinental geography. Still, he reminded himself, Claw was an unusual Indian.

'Yes,' he said, fighting hard to save face, 'in the English land, where medicine is a mighty art.'

Claw cut his words short by the simple expedient of waving the metal hook that represented his left hand in a flashing arc through the flames of the campfire.

'I know about the art,' he grated, turning to Natchez and

tapping him with the good hand. 'Tell him.'

Natchez took up the story with relish, his poor command of English overcome by the excitement of his father's story.

'When your people fought amongst themselves,' he intoned as though reciting some religious doctrine, 'the blue-coats fighting the grey ones for the freedom of the blacks in the big war of many cannons, my father fought with the grey people from the land you call Texas. He won many scalps then, scouting for the *confederados*, the grey ones. It was a good war: many whites died. But my father lost his hand when he showed the grey ones a fort built by the blue people. He took them to the place and one of the far-speaking guns, the cannon, exploded near him, the long bullet blew away his hand.'

Beside his son, Claw was nodding in memory.

'He might have died,' Natchez went on, 'but a *médico* saw him and took him away and made the white magic with powder and the little knives that prick like the wasp's sting, and made him alive again.'

Claw grinned, although it might have been a grimace of pain, Jubal could not tell from the wrinkled face, and interrupted Natchez' story.

'It was great medicine. Greater than the mightiest of our shamans could conjure. I felt the hand of death take mine.' He waved the hook as he spoke. 'And I followed down the road, until the greycoat *médico* fought death for my life and won. Oh yes.' He stared hard at Jubal. 'I know about the art.'

He gestured at Natchez to continue.

'When my father was made well again his hand was gone, so the white shaman worked again. That my father Claw should be whole, he made for him a hand of metal, stronger than flesh and blood and bone. A hand that is a weapon. A hand that can rip the heart from a man's body. The hand that gave him his name. Claw!'

The exclamatory ending prompted the Apaches to murmur assent of Claw's greatness, as though, thought Jubal, they were uttering 'amen' at the end of a prayer.

'But now,' he said quickly, 'the great Claw is hurt again.'

The Apache chief nodded his agreement, his good right hand going involuntarily to the red stain on the front of his blanket.

Jubal seized advantage of the moment.

'And who will heal him now?'

Claw looked up at Jubal, the little dark eyes peering shrewdly from the lines networking his face.

'You say you are a doctor?' he demanded.

'Yes,' replied Jubal evenly, 'I am.'

'Then you will heal me,' Claw announced calmly.

'I can try.' Jubal had his opportunity now, but he knew he must approach it cautiously. 'It will not be easy here.' He indicated the camp with a wave of his hand.

The Apache's hook slashed down, gouging the earth and he coughed more blood.

'Yes,' he grunted, 'you can try. And if you do not, you will die very slowly.'

'And what,' Jubal asked, 'if you should die? I am a doctor, but I cannot work miracles.'

'If I die,' Claw said calmly, 'you will follow me. Natchez will see to it. If you save me, then you will live to face the run of the arrow.'

'Heads,' muttered Jubal, 'you win. Tail, I lose.'

Across the fire, Kincaid laughed, a grating sound filled with pure malice. Vicious amusement shone in his black eyes as he stared at Jubal.

'C'mon, Cade,' he grinned, 'what you got to lose? Except your life, o' course, an' right now that ain't worth a good goddam.'

Jubal came close then to throwing everything away in one desperate attempt to get to the killer. Instinctively, his legs tensed for a dive forward, his hands flexing in anticipation of closing around Kincaid's throat. The man sensed the pent-up fury in Jubal's body, for his right hand moved towards the butt of the matched Colt hung on his thigh as his sneer dared Jubal to make the try.

Shuddering with the sheer tension of the moment, Jubal forced himself to think logically. To attack now would be insane: he had no chance. Better, then, to wait, take the long gamble he had worked out in offering to operate on the Indian chief, hoping it would win him some kind of goodwill with the Apaches. Hope to survive the ordeal that must follow. And then – he savoured the thought – kill Kincaid. Calm now, and cold with controlled anger, he stared back.

'It just might be worth more than yours,' he grated, his eyes probing Kincaid's face with such ferocity that the bigger man looked away.

'White men talk too much,' Natchez interrupted the visual duel. 'You come now.'

He shoved Jubal back away from the fire, steering him towards the encircling hogans as he demanded to know what his captive would need for the forthcoming medical work.

The Apache dwellings were neither well-lit enough, nor sufficiently sanitary, to offer Claw much chance of surviving what could be a delicate operation; and in consequence, they represented a threat to Jubal's own survival. Instead, knowing it was a dangerous chance to take, he opted to work in the open. Backed by Natchez' authority, he arranged for blankets to be washed and dried before the fresh-stoked campfires. A group of complaining warriors was detailed to construct a rough operating table, using whatever wood they could find, then Jubal scrubbed it with whiskey commandeered from Kincaid's protesting henchmen.

By the time the preparations were finished the sun was coming up over the cliffs and Jubal was demanding coffee. So long, he thought, as he could command the situation, he would make himself as comfortable as possible.

He waited until the sun was throwing clear light down over the camp and then sent for Claw.

Four braves lifted the old chief onto the impromptu table and Jubal poured the better part of a bottle of whiskey down his throat. Then he administered chloroform from his valise; there was not enough to keep Claw unconscious throughout the operation and Jubal was hoping that the whiskey and anaesthetic together would produce the desired effect.

It seemed to, for Claw grunted happily and slumped flat on the newly-laundered blanket, his lips parted in an inane grin.

Swiftly, Jubal stripped him to the waist and began to wash his torso and stomach clean of the clotted blood and grease that coated his upper body. When he was satisfied that he had removed all that would come off, Jubal took a long probe and bent over the Apache's stomach.

He inserted the slender metal rod in the hole left by the bullet and began, gently, to seek out the deadly lead. Claw was drunk and drugged, and ropes held his limbs to the table, but it still took four heavily built Apaches to hold him down as

59

Jubal probed for the metal.

Ideally, Jubal knew, the whole thing should have been done under proper surgical conditions. Full anaesthetic and a complete opening up of the outer stomach were what was called for. As things stood he had no choice but to rely on the whiskey and his own skill with probe and forceps. And, he reminded himself, a strong dose of pure luck. One thing in his favour, however, was the sheer resilience of the old Indian. Unlike most white men, he was accustomed to suffering pain, would suffer it stoically and ultimately stand a better chance of surviving it. Jubal hoped that he was not over-estimating that factor, for his own life depended upon it.

He lost track of time as he worked, pausing only to press the chloroform-soaked cloth over Claw's nose and mouth whenever the Indian looked like regaining full consciousness. Natchez stood close by his elbow, silent and watchful, a rifle held ominously in his folded arms.

Deft and delicate, Jubal used the forceps to poke down into the wound, relying on his sense of touch to locate and fasten onto the bullet. Sweat ran unnoticed down his face, just as the sun ran unnoticed across the sky and the watching Indians faded away into a vague blur in the background of his vision. His entire concentration was focused upon the task in hand, to the exclusion of all extraneous happenings.

It was a faculty vital to any successful surgeon; to possess the ability to dismiss from the mind anything that was not immediately relevant to the operation. To concentrate completely, oblivious to anything else.

Jubal possessed that faculty. It made him a good doctor and it helped save his life.

He never heard the sigh that went up around him as he withdrew the dripping, red forceps and dropped the blunted lump of lead onto the grass. He never heard Natchez' sharp intake of his breath, or Kincaid's muttered curse as he washed the wound again and sewed it closed. He never saw the admiring glances of the Apaches as he bandaged the old chief and gave orders for him to be carried, still resting on the makeshift table, back to his hogan.

Natchez listened gravely to Jubal's instructions for Claw's post-operative care, passing on the white man's words to the listening squaws who bustled around the supine body of the chief. Jubal watched them hurrying towards the hogan that contained Claw's unconscious form and hoped that they obeyed his instructions instead of reverting to Apache medicine.

As he watched, something intruded upon his senses and he realized suddenly that he was very hungry. The smells of food cooking were producing anticipatory reactions in his stomach and he looked at the Hunter watch slung across his vest front. He had been working on Claw for five hours, the sun had risen and crossed the sky and it was now gone noon.

Abruptly, Jubal realized that he was tired and hungry, in need of food and sleep.

He waited, under the watchful eyes of impassive Apache guards, until Natchez returned from seeing to his father and asked the young man if he could eat. His medical expertise had obviously raised his status above that of the ordinary captive, for Natchez—clearly now in command during his father's absence—gave immediate orders, so that Jubal was led away to a nearby fire and offered a bowl of stew.

Natchez joined him, hunkering down as though they were two old friends, and gestured at the waiting woman. Jubal's bowl was filled a second time and he devoured it hungrily, ignoring the rancid smell of grease, waiting for Natchez to say something.

'You a good doctor,' grunted the young Indian around a lump of gristly meat. 'If my father lives, maybe you will too.'

Jubal grinned, in spite of his predicament. 'Some doctors would charge a fee,' he said, wondering if Natchez would understand, 'me, I just do it for the love of life.'

Natchez understood.

'Whose?' He grunted. 'My father's or yours?'

'Make a stupid statement,' muttered Jubal ruefully, 'and you get a sensible answer.'

# CHAPTER TEN

For three days Jubal's life hung in precarious balance as Claw fought to survive. That he had succeeded so far in his struggle was in itself a tribute to the old man's tenacity, but the wound, pain and time had told on even his rugged body; right now, Jubal knew, it was touch and go.

In many ways, he was grateful for the respite: he doubted that he could have won the run of the arrow in his own wounded condition. At least the delay gave him a chance to build his strength, resting and exercising until, on the third day, he felt like a new man. During the time he was forced to stay around the rancheria he came to know Natchez—at least, he felt, as well as any white man could ever get to know an Apache. The young war chief made a special point of keeping Jubal and Kincaid apart, often intervening when Kincaid's taunts threatened to provoke a violent reaction from the prisoner. Jubal came to realize that, ruthless though they undoubtedly were, the Apaches were not entirely at fault in the current troubles. They had been driven out of the Salt River territory by the Army, a 'cleaning' operation designed to leave the hills clear for mining. Dumped on a reservation too small and too poor to support them, they had broken out, returning to their traditional lands only to find the area filled with miners. They had reacted in the only way they knew how. Now they were fighting a running war, supported by Lee Kincaid and his renegades.

Natchez obviously had little respect for his white allies, but tolerated them for the guns they could supply. It was an uneasy partnership and Jubal wondered if he could use the uneasiness to his own advantage.

Meanwhile, however, he had Claw to worry about.

For a day and a half, the chief hung between life and death, with the scales ready to tip in either direction. Then he began to rally. He emerged from the delirium that had gripped him shouting for food and Jubal knew he was on the way to recovery. The next day, he wanted to get up and it took all the persuasive powers of Natchez and Jubal to keep him stretched on his blanket bed.

It was another week before Jubal deemed the old man fit enough to rise, and Claw was torn between admiration of his prisoner's skill and resentment of his unorthodox position in the camp.

'You are a good healer,' he grunted, leaning heavily on Natchez' arm as he paced slowly through the rancheria, 'and I thank you for what you have done. But you are also a prisoner, and the law is clear: you must still face the test.'

'I reckoned on that,' Jubal said evenly, 'just like I reckon on winning it.'

Claw cackled his appreciation, clutching at the bandages wrapping his stomach when the pain of laughing hit him.

'Cade,' he approved, 'you would make a good Apache.'

Natchez grunted his assent as Jubal wondered at the sheer incongruity of the situation. It was, he mused, more like being a guest than a prisoner.

The feeling did not last long, for now that Claw was back on his feet there was no reason to delay the test any further. Kincaid was delighted when, at the evening meal, Claw announced the run would take place the next day. The chief designated four warriors, Natchez amongst them, as Jubal's pursuers, then permitted Kincaid to join in, too.

Jubal quit the meeting early: he wanted all the rest he could get.

Come morning, he was up before the sun, shivering in the dawn cold as he headed, flanked by two sleepy-eyed guards, for the nearest fire. Early as it was, Natchez was there before him, black eyes staring impassively at Jubal.

He motioned Jubal to a place beside him and began to speak, slowly, carefully.

'It is no longer my wish to kill you. When first I took you prisoner, I thought you another white-eyes miner come to spoil our land. Now, though, I know you for a brave man and a great healer. If it were not for you, my father would be dead; for that I asked for your life. But my father has told me the Apache law which cannot be broken, so you must make the run and I must hunt you. I have thought long about this and I know now that I do not wish to kill you.' He paused, staring hard at Jubal. 'I shall though, if I must. Run swift, brother, so

63

that I need not take your life.'

It was the longest speech Jubal had heard him make, and he had, even through the stoic lines of the young warrior's face, some idea of the difficulty Natchez must have had in making it. Instinctively, he reached out to grasp the Apache's forearm.

'Natchez,' he said evenly, 'I value what you say, and I shall run fast. But if you catch me, I shall fight and, if I must, I shall kill you.'

Natchez grinned, nodding his head in appreciation.

'Good. We understand one another. Let it be so, and may the spirit of the swift pony be with you.'

Jubal was about to reply when a voice from behind interrupted.

'Well, ain't this just dandy.'

Jubal turned, recognizing Kincaid's voice. The scarfaced man was standing behind and to one side, a mocking smile fixed on his face.

'Ole Natchez here may not be about to kill you, Cade, but I'll tell you true, if I get up to you, you're finished. Bet on it.'

A smile like a death's head creased Jubal's face into a furious facsimile of humour. The scar tissue across the bridge of his nose stood out white against his tan as the skin stretched taut over his cheekbones. His nostrils flared as his blazing eyes probed Kincaid's face, the raw hatred in them sending the killer a pace backwards.

'Kincaid,' the name came out of Jubal's mouth as though he was spitting nails, 'you won't have to catch up to me. I'll be waiting for you. Killing you is going to be a real pleasure.'

The Apache guards did not speak English, but the tenor of the brief conversation, and the animosity blazing between the two white men, were such that their rifles came up to bear on Jubal and Kincaid in anticipation of trouble.

Once again, Natchez intervened.

'Kincaid,' he grunted, rising to his feet, so that he stood eye to eye with the tall gunman, 'the killing time is later. Not now. Go back to your own people.'

The scarfaced murderer looked for a moment as though he would pick a fight, but then he took control of himself, spat into the dust, and spun on his heel. Whistling tunelessly, he walked away to where his men were beginning to prepare breakfast. Watching him go, Jubal fought hard for control of the burning need to destroy the man there and then, regardless of the consequences. He knew that any attack would drive the Apaches to gun him down, but the temptation was fierce. Then he thought of Andy, back in the St. Louis clinic, and the youngster's dependence on the money he sent back to Professor Lenz. Bitterly, he forced himself to stay seated, to let the killing rage pass. Slowly, calm returned; there would be, he promised himself, ample opportunity to kill Kincaid during the test.

The thought sustained him as he prepared for the trial.

The whole rancheria turned out to watch the start, a column of shuffling figures following Claw, sitting heavily on a pinto pony, out of the hidden canyon. They walked for a half-mile until they came to an open space dotted with mesquite and scattered with small boulders. Jubal estimated that it ran for about a quarter-mile before dropping away into broken terrain where ravines and twisted piñon trees offered a degree of cover. The drop was steep and beyond it the country got worse, tumbled rock formations cragging up in weird configurations like solidified cloud castles. If, Jubal thought to himself, he could stay ahead of the pack as far as the escarpment, then he might just stand a chance.

In a few moments his wonderings were put to the test.

Claw tossed him a heavy-bladed Bowie knife as the four Apaches and Kincaid stripped to the waist. All five pursuers were wearing moccasins and carrying knives. Natchez looked unhappy, but the others were grinning in wolfish anticipation of the hunt. Jubal pulled off his jacket and handed it, together with the grey derby and his vest, to an Indian standing close by Claw's mustang. The gold Hunter he entrusted to the chief.

'Don't worry,' he smiled with more assurance than he felt. 'I'll be back to get it.'

Claw nodded, whether in sympathy, agreement or mockery, Jubal couldn't tell, and summoned up a bowman.

The Apache was carrying a four-foot horn bow and a single arrow. He walked out in front of the crowd and notched the shaft; Claw ushered Jubal forward to stand alongside and then grunted a command. The archer drew back the bowstring, lifting the heavy metal head of the arrow skywards. When the string reached his shoulder, he let fly.

The arrow arced high up into the morning air, a slender, humming thing that carried Jubal's life on its point.

It landed a little over halfway across the flatland. Jubal ran towards it.

He ran easily, not hurrying, taking care not to panic or wind himself. He wished that he had a sheath for the knife, for its weight in his right hand threw him slightly off balance so that he had to compensate in his stride. But he reached the arrow unhampered and in good wind, and threw himself into a spurt towards the rocky ground ahead.

Behind him, he heard a great yell go up; although he did not bother to look round at the five figures racing after him, he knew that the contest was now in earnest.

He hit the edge of the plateau at a full run, feeling ground give way to empty space beneath his feet. For a long moment he was in the air, falling feet-first down the slope. Then his boot-heels hit dirt and he allowed the momentum of his passage to carry him on down, arms flailing in a desperate attempt to maintain balance. The attempt succeeded and he reached the bottom of the slope as the first pursuer came over the ridge. Jubal heard a yell behind him and concentrated on finding cover amongst the boulders and piñons, hoping to throw the hunters off his trail.

Panting now, he jinked between the big rocks, taking care to keep a boulder at his back whenever he made a turn. He pushed the pace for ten more minutes then stopped, his breath coming in long gasps as he sank to his knees, pulling air into lungs pushed close to their limit.

He was careful to keep his breathing as quiet as possible, listening at the same time for any sound of pursuit.

The hunters were less careful, coming down the escarpment in a hail of falling shale, yelling as they ran, spacing out as the swifter runners drew ahead.

Jubal rose to his feet and loped on for ten more minutes. Then he stopped again and began to climb to a vantage point atop a crenellated rock. The jagged edges of the boulder afforded him sufficient cover to peer out over his backtrail without being spotted. He saw two Apaches coming up fast, well ahead of the others, but separated by several hundred feet as they cast amongst the rocks for their quarry.

He grinned mirthlessly and slid down off the boulder, gripping the Bowie knife edge uppermost. Silently, like a stalking cat, he moved towards a junction with the foremost Indian.

Wolf Runner was the acknowledged champion of the tribe's foot-racers. He could outrun anyone he knew; and he was confident that he could outrun the small white man ahead of him. Equally, he was confident that he could take the white eyes' scalp. He enjoyed the run of the arrow: it was good sport and the three runs he had made before had given him great prestige when he returned waving the bloody hair of his victim. Today promised to be equally satisfying.

Wolf Runner was very surprised when the small white man suddenly materialized from behind a large rock and stuck a Bowie knife deep into his stomach. He would have screamed if Jubal's knee had not smashed the sound back down his throat, but he was twisting over the pain in his belly and the knee came up very fast and very hard, so that he fell silently, his own knife dropping from numbing fingers.

Then he didn't feel anything at all, except – briefly – the stabbing pain of the blade that sank into his heart.

With a soft *whoomp* of exhaled air, Wolf Runner gave up his final race as Jubal made off on a diagonal path that would lead him ahead of the next hunter.

Walks-His-Pony was so named for his boast that in battle he could walk his pony away from the enemy knowing that he could out-run anyone who came after him, even though on foot. He was the second fastest runner in Claw's band; now, with Wolf dead, the fastest. He was more careful than his fellow warrior, watching the ground ahead for sign of ambush as he loped on after the obstinate little white man who was already much farther into the badlands than any other had got.

He saw Jubal as the snarling figure powered itself from the cover of a tall cactus, Bowie knife cutting savagely for the Apache's stomach. With a practised movement, Walks-His-Pony jinked sideways and sucked in his belly, so that Jubal's thrust left only a faint traceline of blood across his midriff. At the same time, he swung his own knife in a vicious arc that would have buried the blade deep in Jubal's neck had he still been in the line of cut. But he wasn't. Instead, he was rolling to one side, using the momentum of his blow to carry him past the Indian.

In a single, clean movement he spun around, right arm extended to parry the next blow. It came in hard and fast, riding up over the top of Jubal's blade to carve a scarlet line across his bicep.

Pain and the knowledge that the Apache facing him was a far better knife-fighter flooded simultaneously through Jubal's senses. He made a swiftly dangerous decision and threw his knife straight at the warrior's face.

He was no knife thrower, and the blade twirled harmlessly through the air, hitting grip-first against the Indian's face. But it gave him the advantage he wanted: Walks-His-Pony paused involuntarily, ducking his head to avoid the whirling knife.

Jubal grabbed that tiny advantage and powered himself forward in a straight dive at the man's stomach. As his head cannoned into flesh, he felt a stabbing pain high in his back that told him his opponent's blade had been turned to stab him. He ignored it as he landed on top of the Indian and brought his knees up in a vicious drive that rammed hard into the Apache's groin.

Walks-His-Pony screamed as agony lanced up through his gut and butted his head in an attempt to smash Jubal's nose. He failed, for the white demon turned his head, taking the blow on his left cheek, and rolled over, grabbing the Indian's right wrist as he went. Walks-His-Pony was suddenly conscious of a boot driven hard against his skull, and of another resting against his armpit. Then he felt an awful pressure wrenching at his arm, dragging all feeling from his right hand, so that his fingers went dead and the knife slipped from his grasp. A strange calm enveloped him as he felt his arm torn from its socket to dangle uselessly by his side. It overrode even the agony that drenched his body in sudden sweat and, with a dreadful clarity, he recognised that he was about to die. He began to open his mouth to sing his death song, but Jubal's fist stopped him. It hammered against his teeth, driving shards of stained ivory down his throat, cutting off the chant before it could start. Then another fist landed on his windpipe, blocking air from his lungs as his Adam's apple caved in.

Jubal sprang to one side as the choking Indian's body assumed a foetal position, its first and last stance in life, and began to run. The Apache dying behind him and the one he had knifed leavened the odds a little. Now there were only three men after him, he wanted to build up some distance again, enough to pause and plan the next ambuscade.

Breathing deeply and trying hard to control his pounding heart, he ran through the maze of rock and piñon trees. A howl told him that one of the bodies had been discovered: he concentrated on keeping his advantage.

He succeeded, staying ahead of his pursuers for the remainder of the day. He was badly winded, his breath coming in sharp, rasping gasps as the sun went down behind the rim of the mesa, but he was still alive. And still ahead of the hunt.

He kept on running, willpower rather than strength moving his legs, until it was almost too dark to see. Several times, he stumbled over rocks or fallen branches and sprawled headlong on the dusty ground, but he pushed himself forward until the fading light and his aching body told him to stop. When he did, he was in an open area of sandy ground, flanked on two sides by jumbled boulders and on the third by a thicket of cactus plants. The spiky stems rose to more than twice a man's height, presenting a formidable barrier of out-thrusting spines. Jubal dropped to the ground and wriggled hazardously between the main stems. As he had hoped, he found a clear space at the centre, small, but sufficiently open to permit him to stretch out in a semblance of comfort. He could ill afford to move in his sleep for fear of impaling himself, but the vegetative fortress offered the best cover he could hope to find.

He used the Bowie knife to slice a minor branch from one of the plants and sucked gratefully on the sour-tasting juice that oozed from the cut end; it was the first drink he had had since morning.

When he had slaked his thirst, Jubal tossed the cactus limb aside and settled down to sleep. He was too weary to worry about the discomfort of his position and simply thrust the knife into the sand, close by, where he could reach it easily, before pillowing his head on his left arm and passing out.

The cackling of the buzzards woke him, lifting him up out of sleep into instantaneous awareness, the knife gripped and ready to use. But the birds were just watching, perched on the cactus branches, hoping for an easy breakfast. Jubal disappointed them by rising to his knees to cut another

69

thirst-quenching stem, sending the black-pinioned scavengers squawking up in panicked circles towards the rising sun.

The lifting column of birds reminded him simultaneously of the deadly hunt in which he was the quarry, and of the immediate danger they represented.

In the early morning light, the wheeling shapes were a clear indication of his position, pinpointing him as exactly as any sticker in a map. His pursuers could not fail to miss the birds any more than they could fail to guess that a moving thing had spooked them. And the only thing moving right then was Jubal.

He wriggled out of the thicket faster than he had gone in, checked his backtrail, and set out again at a steady lope.

Behind him the Apache called Little Eagle sprang to his feet, his keen ears alert to the alarm cries of the birds. He was used, from the many war-raids he had ridden on, to sleeping rough and coming instantly awake; equally, he was used to using natural signs to pin-point an enemy. The flight of a buzzard, the run of a prairie dog, the trail of a snake, all meant something to Little Eagle. Wolf Runner or Walks-His-Pony might be faster on foot, but there was no warrior in Claw's band – not even Natchez – who could track better than Little Eagle.

As soon as he saw the rising of the black wings, he knew where the white man was and set out after him.

Where Natchez and the other white man might be, he neither knew nor cared. The white-eyes out in front was what he wanted. Wolf Runner had been his brother and now Wolf was dead, killed by the little white *médico* who had no right to be still alive.

Little Eagle pushed a strip of water-soaked rawhide, drenched in the morning's dew, between his teeth and began to run.

He ran for several hours, his powerful legs pumping distance between him and Jubal, before he picked up clear sign. Then he could see the scuffed sand and the tatters of cloth caught on cactus thorns that told him he was on the right trail. Soon, from the depth of the footprints and the heat difference between the indentation and the out-lying ground, he knew he was closing on his brother's killer. He pulled the dried rawhide from between his teeth, tucked the strip into his belt, and quickened his pace.

All morning he had been alone, and he hoped it would stay that way. He did not want Natchez or Kincaid to find the white-eyes *bastardo* first; he wanted the pleasure of the killing to be his alone, in revenge for Wolf Runner.

With the measured breath of a trained Apache warrior, he pushed himself faster along the white man's trail, closing the distance with long, loping strides.

Up ahead Jubal had come to the conclusion that he could not hope to outrun the Apaches. Kincaid, his main concern, was another matter, but before he could get to grips with Mary's killer, he knew he would have to handle Natchez and the other Indian. The sun was peaking at its noon zenith when he slowed and began to circle back along his trail.

He had no real idea of where his followers might be, but he assumed that they would be coming along his own path so that a parallel track in the opposite direction would bring him into contact.

It did, much sooner than he had anticipated.

He was moving slow and silent through the screening back-drop of cacti and mesquite when he saw Little Eagle moving fast but cautious through the scrub. The Apache was studying the ground with practised eyes, tailing Jubal's track as straight as a hound-dog on a game trail.

It was that single-minded dedication that caused Little Eagle to miss Jubal and gave Jubal the advantage.

He waited until the Apache came up alongside him before exploding from the side of the trail like a human cannon ball. Coming out fast and clean in a run that smashed his left shoulder hard against the Indian's back, Jubal gave himself time to swing his knife downwards in a long, cutting stroke that split skin in a gaping wedge across the shoulders of the stumbling warrior.

The run carried him on and over the fallen man, so that he had time to turn, knife raised, before Little Eagle rolled to his feet. Pure hate glowed in the Apache's eyes as he moved to-wards Jubal; he ignored the blood running down his back as he shifted his knife in a weaving, light-shafting pattern before him.

Wolf Runner had been his younger brother, and the Runner was dead: killed by this small white-eyes against all odds.

71

Now Little Eagle would rectify the score.

He came on with death his companion, raw slaughter glinting from the edge of his blade.

Jubal saw the fanaticism written across the warrior's normally impassive features and began to circle away from the rocks at his back towards the open space at the trail's centre.

Little Eagle's first cut he parried with a dull ringing from his knife blade. The second stroke left a tracery of blood over his shirtfront. The third would have gutted him had he not powered himself sideways, so that the wicked edge was deflected by his left forearm, his shirt sleeve turning scarlet as he hit the ground off to one side.

Ignoring the pain, Jubal rolled clean and mean to his feet as Little Eagle hurled himself forward for the killing blow. His target, however, was not there. Instead, Jubal's right foot came up in a savage kick that blasted air from the Indian's chest, stopping him for a moment in his tracks. Jubal seized the moment to deliver a slashing stroke aimed at the Apache's throat. Little Eagle was too fast, though, and the cut landed on his chest as he threw himself back onto the sand.

Before he could roll or rise, Jubal was moving towards him, kicking hard at the flailing legs that were trying to keep him away. It was a savage contest, Apache in-fighting pitted against Jubal's knowledge of Chicago street-wars. And the Apache won the first round.

He knocked Jubal's feet out from underneath him, sprawling the white man heavily onto his back. Before Jubal could rise, Little Eagle was up on his feet, one moccasin-clad foot lashing out to knock the Bowie knife from his opponent's hand to fall far away in the scrub.

With a triumphant yell he made his big mistake as he threw himself down on the fallen white-eyes, blade extended for the killing thrust.

This kind of fighting Jubal was more used to than knife work. He lifted his feet as Little Eagle came down on him, planting both boots hard into the Apache's stomach. At the same time he shifted his head and torso sideways to avoid the knife, wrapping both hands around the Indian's wrist as the blade came down, pulling on the arm as he kicked his legs straight.

Little Eagle yelled again, this time in sheer surprise as he

72

felt himself lifted high into the air on the tail-end of a mule-like kick. Then he screamed as he landed: Jubal held onto his arm so that it snapped at the elbow as the man fell.

Any ordinary fighter would have given up, but Little Eagle was an Apache and Wolf Runner had been his brother. He snarled, picked up the knife in his left hand, and came back to the attack.

Jubal ducked to one side as a wild swing whistled close over the top of his head and leaped forward, one leg thrust out to ram into the Indian's belly. Little Eagle coughed hard and fell backwards at the same time that Jubal measured his length on the sand. The white man was the first back on his feet, this time avoiding the kicks of his enemy. Instead, he scooped a handful of sand and hurled it at Little Eagle's face. Blinded and confused, the Apache was barely aware of the body that crashed down on him, rock-hard elbows smashing against his ribs so that bone splintered in lung-puncturing shards.

Jubal rolled off to one side as gobbets of blood exploded from the Apache's lips, and kicked out again, driving the tip of his right boot hard against Little Eagle's knee.

He felt the knee-cap shatter under the blow, lifting another agonized scream from the warrior's mouth, as he reached over to pluck the knife from his hand.

Deft and clean, and as coolly as a butcher in a slaughter-house, Jubal drew the razor-edged blade across Little Eagle's throat.

The screaming stopped as the blood-flow increased, the Apache choking on his own life-essence. Jubal felt warm red-ness spatter against his face and pushed himself back to avoid the spuming fountain that poured from Little Eagle's severed throat.

Then he rose up and started to run again. He was deep into the badlands now, and beginning to feel the muscle-straining effects of the long hours of running and fighting. Deliberately, he slowed his pace, moving cautiously through the tangled scrub. Natchez and Kincaid could be anywhere in the wasteland of jumbled rock and stunted trees and there was little point in moving blindly forward. Jubal's gear was back at the Apache camp and he had no intention of leaving it there. He planned to end the hunt – one way or another – and return.

No more running, he decided; instead he would find a defensive position and let his pursuers come to him.

The search was ended abruptly by a cliff that fell away almost from beneath Jubal's feet. It was as though a gigantic knife had sliced a great chunk out of the ground, a sheer drop that fell a couple of hundred feet to the canyon below. Jubal pulled himself up on the very edge, grabbing a piñon branch to keep his balance. The cliff was hidden from sight by the trees growing along its edge and Jubal drew back into their cover as he began to work his way along the rim.

He was moving silently through the undergrowth, hoping to intersect Natchez' or Kincaid's path, when a shot crashed through the still afternoon air.

Splinters blasted from a tree to Jubal's left as he hurled himself to the ground, seeking cover behind the trunk.

A second shot threw dirt up into his face and he crabbed sideways, trying to get out of the line of fire. Four explosions coming in rapid succession followed his path, marking it with rising dust clouds, forcing Jubal to realize that the hidden marksman held him under a clear field of fire.

Then a shout brought a curse to his lips.

'Cade! I told you I'd get you. You're dead meat.'

Somewhere out in the brush Kincaid was stalking him with a Winchester.

# CHAPTER ELEVEN

Jubal concentrated on finding cover. Kincaid was obviously playing with him, for the rifle could have blasted life from his body any time the scarfaced man had wanted. Counting on Kincaid's innate sadism to keep him playing deadly games, Jubal took a long chance and came up on his feet. There was an uneasy prickling running the length of his spine as he waited for a bullet to hit, but he ignored it as he powered himself sideways, diving for a gap between two trees.

He landed on hands and knees, rolled so that the piñons were to either side of him and then hurled himself deeper into the thicket.

Shots echoed behind him, ploughing furrows along the protecting branches, but Kincaid had lost his initial advantage; he no longer held Jubal under clear sight.

Jubal began to move around in the direction of the last shot. It was hard going through the brush and he was forced to wriggle on his belly through the denser patches, thorns tearing at hands and face to leave bloody lines wherever flesh was exposed. But he ignored the pain in his determination to reach Kincaid. He could hear the man moving cautiously around the thicket, trying to spot his quarry. It was fruitless for the trees were far too closely spaced to permit a clear view.

Kincaid decided to forgo caution and triggered three shots at random. None came near Jubal, but they served to remind him that even though he was hidden, Kincaid still carried the advantage of a .44 Winchester.

Warily, Jubal moved to the thinning edge of the undergrowth and peered out. From his prone position, his line of sight was severely limited so that it was the sound of Kincaid's voice that pinpointed the killer. He was standing close by a piñon, the Winchester cradled ready to fire, eyeing the thicket nervously. About nine feet of broken ground separated him from Jubal and it was obvious that Jubal had no chance of rushing him. Quietly, he withdrew into the brush and began to move to a better vantage point.

He got to within five feet of the man he had been hunting for so long, and was tensing his legs to plunge forward when Kincaid turned. Whether it was his gunman's sixth sense or some faint sound that Jubal had made it was impossible to tell, but as Jubal powered himself from the brush, the ugly black muzzle of the Winchester swung around in his direction.

Kincaid's face split in a wolfish smile of anticipation as he squeezed the trigger. The muzzle flash burned Jubal's face and he felt a sickening blow smash pain deep into his skull. A flash of red blinded him as a great roaring filled his ears and numbness froze his muscles. The momentum of his leap carried him forward, but the hands stretched out to grasp Kincaid no longer felt anything, the fingers clawing nervelessly on empty air.

The gunman stepped to one side as Jubal collapsed on the sand. A smear of sticky red blood showed beneath his head as he lay still and supine.

'Like I said,' snarled Kincaid, 'you're dead meat.'

He levered the action of the Winchester and pressed the barrel against the back of Jubal's neck. His finger was tightening on the trigger when a second figure exploded from the brush.

'No!' Natchez' shout stopped Kincaid, who swung the rifle over to cover the warrior.

Natchez stood shaking with rage, his knife held ready to use, his left hand pointing accusingly at the white man.

'Kincaid, you break the law of the run. Hunter and quarry, all carry knives. Guns are forbidden.'

'Gee, Natchez,' mockery sounded in the reply, 'guess I felt like I wanted a bit more on my side. Always did favour a stacked deck.' The mocking note left his voice, to be replaced by cold deadliness. 'Now back off, injun, or I'll blow you to hell along with Cade.'

The anger shaking Natchez' body erupted into violent action. With a snarl he swung his right hand up in an underarm movement that sent his knife flashing at Kincaid's throat.

Instinctively, the white man raised the Winchester and triggered a shot. The bullet shattered the whirling blade before it could do any damage, but before the killer was able to lever another round into the chamber, Natchez had closed with him.

They were both big men, lean and tough and used to dirty fighting. What Natchez gained from a lifetime of Indian wrestling, Kincaid matched with brute strength. He swung the Winchester in a clubbing movement that sent a shock of pain along the arm Natchez used to deflect the blow. Then he was too close for the gun to be any use and Kincaid dropped it, grappling bare-handed with the Indian.

Natchez' anger gave him additional strength, but the food Kincaid's men had sneaked him along with the rifle meant he was in better shape than the hungry Apache and it began to tell as they fought across the open space.

Kincaid knocked Natchez' arms away from his throat and kneed the Indian hard in the groin. The young Apache moaned and dropped his guard long enough for the white man to drive a fist into his mouth. Natchez staggered backwards as Kincaid rained blows at his face, and tripped awkwardly on gnarled root.

As he went down, Jubal came to. The side of his head felt as though a hot poker was pressed against his temple where the bullet had grazed him and he had to blink several times before the double vision cleared. Sledgehammers seemed to be pounding at the walls of his skull and he could taste bile in his mouth. But he was still clear-headed enough to sum up the situation with a single quick glance. Natchez was obviously losing the fight – though why the two men were trying to kill one another, Jubal could not guess – and Kincaid appeared to be weaponless. Jubal's eyes darted over the impromptu arena, seeking the rifle. When he spotted the gun he found his legs were too shaky to stand up, so he began to crawl towards it.

Kincaid was hammering at Natchez with a broken branch when Jubal reached the Winchester. He shook his head as he picked it up, wondering why it should be so heavy, and cocked the hammer. Painfully, he pushed himself up to a sitting position and brought the rifle to his shoulder.

He was sighting on Kincaid's chest when Natchez kicked the man backwards. Jubal lost his target and swore as the rolling bodies blocked his aim. He was tempted to pump slugs at random into both men, but could not bring himself to kill Natchez so needlessly.

In any event, it appeared that Kincaid had done it for him. The scarfaced man punched Natchez low in the belly and

77

kicked him as he doubled over. The Apache was knocked backwards and stood with his arms flailing madly in some crazy impersonation of a bird. A look of blank surprise appeared on his face and he opened his mouth to emit a wild cry as he pitched over the edge of the cliff.

As Natchez disappeared from sight, Jubal fired the Winchester. The bullet took the lobe of Kincaid's right ear with it, but Jubal was too groggy to fire true.

He pumped a second round into the gun as Kincaid turned to run. Then a faint cry came up from below: Jubal could not understand the words, but the sound alone told him that Natchez was still alive. He fired, the shot whistling over Kincaid's head. The killer pushed on through the trees and Jubal found himself caught in a dilemma. All his instincts told him to go after Mary's murderer, leave the Indian to his fate and hunt down the gunman. But a faint pricking of his conscience reminded him that Natchez had saved his life. A few months earlier there would have been no hesitation: Jubal would have dismissed the Apache from his mind. Now, however, he was rendered momentarily motionless, indecisive.

Kincaid took advantage of his confusion, making good his escape through the tangle of trees.

Jubal grunted in disgust and began to move to the rim. Maybe he was getting soft, he thought; or maybe the near-inhuman lust for revenge at any price was dying down. It had driven him for many months and more miles, turning him into an implacable killing machine, as though a part of his soul had been removed along with the life of the girl he loved. Perhaps now he was becoming more human. Either way, he knew what Mary would have wanted him to do.

He set the Winchester close by and looked down the cliff.

Natchez had fallen about fifty feet before hitting an outjutting ledge. The rocky platform had saved his life and broken his legs so that he hung, precariously balanced, clutching a small bush. He looked up at Jubal and shouted in English.

'You have won. It is the way of the test and now you can go free. Kill me and finish it. I would rather a bullet than the fall.'

'You've fallen far enough,' shouted Jubal, 'and I may need the bullet later. Right now I'll try to get you up.'

'You are crazy, Jubal,' called Natchez. 'I would have killed you.'

'But you didn't,' muttered Jubal as he swung himself gingerly over the edge.

The cliff seemed steeper and higher than before and he kept his eyes fixed on the rock in front of his face as he felt for hand and footholds.

It was a difficult climb, and he knew that the way back would be a whole lot worse, but once he had committed himself, he pushed doubt from his mind and concentrated on getting down to the Indian. It could not have taken him longer than a half-hour to reach the ledge, but it seemed like an eternity before his toes touched the rock and he could rest for a while. There was barely sufficient room for the two men and Jubal was forced to stand, spread-eagled against the face as he waited for his heart to slow down.

'Now I'm here,' he grinned to Natchez with far more assurance than he felt, 'we'd better figure how to get you back up.'

Natchez was hurt pretty badly and would be unable to help on the climb back. His face was set in stoic lines, but the pain of his broken legs had lightened his tan by several shades. Jubal hoped that he would not pass out, for he was not sure that he could lift a deadweight onto his back. And it was clear that that was how he would have to carry the Apache. Somehow, he had to strap Natchez onto his back for the upward climb.

He pulled Natchez up into a sitting position, grateful for the iron control that was keeping the young Indian conscious and silent, and pulled the belt from his waist. Then Jubal removed his own belt and unbuttoned his shirt. He squatted awkwardly in front of the Indian, the position forcing him to use one hand to grasp the bush, so that Natchez had to follow his instructions. The Apache pushed Jubal's shirt under his broken legs and knotted the sleeves around Jubal's waist. The rough sling was further supported by one of the belts, the other going around Natchez' chest and looping over Jubal's neck. It would not be easy, and a wrong movement might easily result in the belt strangling Jubal – or rather, he reminded himself, cutting off his air for a moment before he fell – but it was the only configuration that would work. At least it left Natchez' arms free so that he could grab any suitable handholds.

Warily, Jubal stood up, scanning the cliff for the best route. Then, grunting with the effort, he began to climb. Natchez helped where he could, but by the time they had covered a few feet of the ascent Jubal's muscles were lancing pain through his body. The belt around his neck made breathing difficult and the sheer strain brought fresh blood welling from the cut on his temple.

It had seemed a long way down; the return journey was infinitely longer.

Twice, Jubal felt his hands slipping sweatily from the rock and only his strength and pure luck saved him from falling. Halfway up, he began to wonder if he had the strength to finish the climb. His limbs were four columns of agony, his lungs felt as though they might burst and a red mist coloured his vision. But he kept moving, slowly, like a grotesque beetle, heading inch by painful inch for the top.

He had lost all sense of time when he finally thrust a hand over the rim. There was no longer even the sensation of pain in his legs, just an all-embracing numbness pervading his body as he crawled like an automaton over the edge.

He dragged himself back from the rim until there was room enough to roll sideways and free Natchez. For a long time both men lay still, panting heavily as they slowly regained strength.

When he could speak again, Jubal turned to Natchez.

'The next time you get in a fight,' he grinned, 'look before you leap.'

# CHAPTER TWELVE

His wounds and the sheer physical effort of the climb, allied with the punishment of the race, had taken a heavy toll of Jubal's resources. As he set rough splints on Natchez' useless legs he pondered his next move. The hunt had taken him the better part of two days into the badlands and now, considerably weaker than when he started, he had the crippled Apache to worry about. Carrying Natchez back seemed out of the question: by the time they made it, gangrene would probably be stealing his life and, anyway, Jubal was by no means sure he could carry the young Indian that far.

The alternative was to leave Natchez by the cliff and go back for help alone. It was risky with Kincaid somewhere out in the scrub and the prospect, from Natchez' point of view, of one, maybe two nights in the open. But it seemed to be the better chance.

They discussed it briefly before Jubal made the Indian as comfortable as possible beneath a rough shelter of cut branches, placed the rifle by his side and headed north.

He ran at an easy pace, not risking exhaustion as he followed his earlier trail back in the direction of Claw's camp. One hundred loping paces, then one hundred at a walk, Jubal kept it up until the lengthening shadows warned him of approaching sunset. He ignored the nagging ache of hunger that cramped his stomach and the sharper pains from the cuts decorating his body. As night fell he scooped a hollow in the sand between two boulders, grateful for the warmth retained in the ground, and settled down to sleep.

It was fitful rest, and when the moon came up Jubal decided to push on. The pale light outlined the terrain well enough to allow him to move swiftly and the physical action of running served to offset the night chill.

He kept moving as dawn painted the badlands pale gold, sucked on a cactus stem as the noon sun burned his eyes, and collapsed, unable to go farther, as the sun went down.

This time weariness dropped him into deep sleep and he

sprawled on the sand until the heat of the sun on his face woke him. It was past dawn and although his aching body protested the effort, he rose and started to run again. Now his steps were faltering, weaving from side to side of the trail. Several times he sprawled full length as his muscles gave out, but always he got up again, the raw power of his will driving him on.

He lost track of time, not noticing when the sun disappeared from the sky or the moon came out. Hunger and pain became a natural part of his consciousness. All he saw was the trail before him and, flickering through his mind's eye, the images of Natchez and of Kincaid.

The figure that crawled over the rim of the escarpment outside Claw's camp was unrecognizable. The Apache guard who spotted the stumbling, falling man had no idea who he was. Nor could the horsemen sent out to meet him recognize the face beneath its caking of dust and dry blood. The blackened tongue that moved between the blistered lips tried to tell them something, but the sounds were unintelligible, as wild as the staring, reddened eyes.

'Ccclllaaa,' mumbled Jubal, trying hard to get his swollen tongue around the syllables. 'Naaashecch.'

The Apaches couldn't understand him, but they thought Claw would probably want to see this tottering wreck of a man so they hoisted him across a pony and led him into camp.

Claw had adhered to the strict letter of Apache law, so that no riders had been sent out to look for the six missing men even though they had been gone far longer than any previous contestants in the run of the arrow. None the less, he was still worried about Natchez and wondered if the newcomer might be a contestant. He failed to recognize Jubal at first, and it was not until the blood and grime caked over his face had been wiped away that Claw saw, with a shock of surprise, that it was the white man.

'You came back.' Astonishment sounded in his voice.

Jubal swallowed the better part of a canteen of water before he could shape a recognizable reply. 'Yeah,' he said thickly, 'I came back like I said I would.'

'Then you have won.' This time Claw's voice was tinged with sadness. 'Did my son die well?'

'No,' said Jubal shortly, then regretted the abrupt reply as he saw the horror on the old man's face. 'He didn't die at all.'

He drank more water as pure befuddlement showed in Claw's eyes. 'He's out there with two busted legs. I'll show you where if you give me Kincaid.'

'The scarfaced one?' It was a question. 'He has not returned. I thought you had killed him.'

Jubal would have spat if his mouth had contained any saliva. Instead he grunted.

'Then where the hell is he?'

'I do not know,' replied Claw, 'he went out after you with the others. You are the only one to return.'

Once more Jubal saw the scarfaced killer slipping from his grasp and cursed. He began to struggle to his feet, but Claw pushed him gently back to the ground.

'My son,' murmured the chief urgently, 'tell me about my son.'

Jubal explained what had happened, telling Claw where Natchez could be found. Then, as soon as he was sure the Apaches could locate him, he let the welcome sleep of exhaustion drift over him. Claw watched Jubal's unconscious carcase lifted up and carried to his own hogan. He gave instructions to his squaws that the white man was to be bathed and cared for, then he called his warriors around him. Two groups were ordered off into the badlands, the first to seek out Natchez and bring him back, the second to find Kincaid.

'He is to be brought in alive,' announced Claw, 'he belongs to the one called Jubal Cade. His life for my son's.'

His remaining warriors were given quieter instructions and began to drift away in twos and threes, moving casually towards the canvas tents of Kincaid's people. As they approached the white encampment, guns and bows, notched ready to use, appeared in their hands. Taken by surprise, the renegades could only wonder volubly at this sudden enmity, protesting that they were friends of the Apaches.

'You are Kincaid's people,' said Claw sternly, 'and Kincaid tried to kill my son. He broke the Apache law by carrying a rifle, and he broke the law of hospitality when he turned on Natchez. For those things he is to die. Whether you will join him or not, I shall decide soon.'

He turned away as his men stripped the whites of their weapons and herded them off to one side of the canyon where they were held under guard.

Jubal was unaware of this dramatic turn in events, and he stayed that way for the next ten hours. When he awoke he was ravenous and had to force himself to eat only sparingly, knowing what too much food could do to him after the hungry days. His wounds had been cleansed and bandaged and the Apache women had cleaned up his clothes as best they could. When he emerged from the hogan he looked almost his old self, apart from the sunburn on his face and hands. Claw had set out not only his vest and jacket, but also his guns and medical valise: obviously Jubal was now accepted as a friend.

The first thing he saw outside was the grinning face of Natchez, propped up on a litter in the centre of the rancheria, recounting in his own language the story of the hunt. He broke off to wave Jubal over to his side and as the small white man hunkered down, a murmur of approval broke from the watching Indians.

Jubal was anxious for news of Kincaid, but Natchez could offer none. The scarfaced man had disappeared into the badlands like a wraith, not even the tribe's best trackers could find a trace of him, though some were still out looking. It was as though, said Natchez, the man had some kind of magic, a charm to protect his life.

'Yeah,' grunted Jubal bitterly, 'black magic to protect his black soul.'

'My brother,' said Natchez in his guttural English, 'I wish to see him die as much as you. We shall go on looking.'

Jubal thought about it, pondering his best course of action. If the Apache scouts were unable to locate Kincaid, there was little chance of his finding the man. Meanwhile, there was still the question of Andy's keep in the Lenz Clinic – and Jubal was not making money brooding in the Indian camp. He made up his mind and told Natchez he was leaving come morning. The young man accepted it, sending a brave to find Claw and impart the news.

That night there was a feast held in Jubal's honour and for the first time he tasted the fierce alcohol the Apaches called mescal. The Indians appeared to find it as potent as did Jubal and the darkness echoed to their shouts and wild firing.

In the morning, the guards posted to watch Kincaid's men were dead and the renegades gone.

Claw dispatched a party of warriors to hunt for them as

Jubal said goodbye. He was not particularly interested in the outlaws: his concern was with Kincaid. So he watched the hunting party ride out before saddling his own horse and heading back down the trail to the mining camp. Nothing, he realized, had been settled about the disputed territory, but that was not his concern. He shrugged his shoulders and concentrated on the journey ahead.

He took it easy and it was two days before he saw the sprawl of tents and shacks flanking the bank of the Salt River.

He kicked the pinto up to a canter, heading down the road past his own mine towards the grimy little settlement. There were few people on mainstreet, but those who saw him riding in gaped as he went by, staring in disbelief after his grey-suited figure. He reined in outside the Golden Nugget and climbed out of the saddle. Carrying the Spencer in one hand and his medical bag in the other, he pushed through the swing doors and walked up to the bar.

Before he could order a drink a familiar voice echoed behind him.

'Whiskey, Harry. The good stuff.'

'Hi, Fred,' grinned Jubal, turning to face Nolan.

The saloon owner was delighted to see his friend, a broad smile creasing his saturnine features as he snatched the bottle before Harry could pour the shots and ushered Jubal to a table.

'So tell me everything.' He poured the whiskey as he spoke. 'We'd given you up for dead. Figgered the renegades had got you.'

'They did,' said Jubal evenly, enjoying the surprise on Nolan's face, 'but they got a mite more than they bargained for.'

'Do tell,' urged Nolan, and the growing crowd around the table backed his demand.

Jubal took a long swallow of whiskey, a deep breath, and began to recite his adventures in the Mogallons. When he had finished the room was silent.

'Hell,' Nolan murmured, 'an' we persuaded the Army to go in after you.'

'What?' Jubal was instantly alert.

'Yeah. 'Bout three days after you'd gone I rode into Cairo an' geed up the cavalry. They sent a squadron out.' He stopped to sip his drink. 'Got here late yesterday an' rode out

85

this morning round sun-up.'

Suddenly Jubal realized how close he had grown to Nat-chez. From thinking of the young Apache as an enemy, he had come to regard him as a friend. Now he recognized that he had no desire to see the tribe attacked, no matter what they had done in revenge for losing their land.

'But I didn't see them on the trail in,' he said urgently.

'You wouldn't have,' agreed Nolan. 'They took the east trail. Had a couple of Mescalero scouts with them, reckoned they knew where the band would be holed up.' He broke off in surprise as Jubal rose hurriedly to his feet. 'Where in the hell you goin' now?'

'Back,' grunted Jubal tersely.

He pushed through the miners ringing the table, ignoring Nolan's shout as he mounted the pinto and galloped back the way he had come.

# CHAPTER THIRTEEN

Jubal pushed the pinto as hard as he dared back towards Claw's hideout. It occurred to him that some insane fate had seen fit to condemn him to race forever between two places, shuttling back and forth on an endless, pre-ordained track. He hoped the cavalry would be moving slower.

Come midnight he was forced to stop for fear of killing the pony. The animal was badly winded and Jubal had to bed down to give it time to recover. He watered the willing beast and gave up his own bedroll to prevent it taking a chill from the night air. Then he kindled a fire and did his best to stay warm. In the morning, the pinto was moving slower but seemed reasonably well recovered. Even so, it was blowing hard as they approached the Apache stronghold and Jubal spotted the guards on the rimrock.

He came forward cautiously, both hands up in the air, hoping the watchers would recognize him.

They did, waving him on through the defile into the main canyon. Natchez was still stretched on his litter and Claw was seated beside him, looking as surprised as his son to see Jubal again.

'Welcome,' he said, rising to his feet as Jubal jumped from the horse, 'we thought you gone.'

'Yeah,' said Jubal, 'but I got some news for you. The Army's coming up.'

Surprise showed again on Claw's face as he peered at Jubal.

'How will they find us.' He paused ominously. 'Unless someone told them where we are.'

'Maybe someone did,' Jubal answered, 'but not me.' A sudden thought crossed his mind. 'Did you find Kincaid?'

'No.' The possibility of betrayal etched deeper lines across the chief's forehead. 'But would a renegade go to the Army?'

'Does the Army know he's a renegade?' countered Jubal. 'Could just be that he made it to Cairo. Anyway, they're coming and they got Mescalero scouts leading them.'

'Mescalero traitors,' snarled Claw, then turned to shout

orders. 'We shall fight.'

'They'll wipe you out,' Jubal grated, 'take your people and run.'

'No.' Claw's rejection was final. 'We have run enough. Now we shall fight.'

'You're crazy,' Jubal snarled, amazed at the old man's dogged obstinacy, 'there's a squadron of cavalry that'll box you up in here like rats in a trap. You don't stand a chance.'

'Perhaps not.' There was pride in Claw's voice now. 'But we shall die like Apaches. Not rot on a reservation like starving dogs.'

He turned away to watch his warriors taking up positions around the canyon walls. Even Natchez was clutching a rifle as two men hauled his litter to a vantage point overlooking the entrance to the camp.

'Thank you, my friend,' said Claw, placing a hand on Jubal's shoulder, 'I am grateful to you, but now you must go, before your own people kill you for a renegade.'

Jubal saw that he could not persuade the Indian and turned away. He walked over to Natchez and held out his right hand. The warrior grasped it.

'Go in peace, brother.'

'You too,' said Jubal wearily and turned to his horse.

He was climbing into the saddle when an explosion rocked the camp, blowing fountains of earth high into the air. A second and third followed in short order.

The concussion bouncing off the canyon walls hammered against Jubal's eardrums, ringing inside his skull as devastating waves of savage force rocked him on his feet. Dirt, grass and bloody remnants of human beings rained down all around him as adrenalin pumped through his veins, so that objective time seemed slowed, as though the explosions were happening in slow motion. Then the pony, spooked by the attack, squealed shrilly and reared up, dragging Jubal off the ground.

He fought the animal down as he realized that the Army had arrived.

His thoughts were punctuated by more blasts.

'They brought a howitzer.'

Blam!

'How the hell can I stop them?'

Boom!

'Claw's people are going to die.'

Powww!

He was unconscious of the shards of hot metal and pulped flesh spattering over him in his urgent need to prevent the carnage. Even as he swung up onto the saddle of the terrified pinto, he was aware of the Apaches dying all around the bowl of the hideout. The lookouts were obviously dead already, or the cavalry would never have got so close; the men Claw had sent to the rimrock were answering the howitzer's thunder with the ineffectual crackling of their rifles and the even less effective twang of bowstrings. The Army was intent on wiping out the hostile Indians. And – it looked like – Jubal, too.

He dragged the pinto round, straining on the reins to force the beast where he wanted it to go, instead of bolting in terror, and headed straight and fast at the entrance to the canyon, hoping to get out and speak before the slaughter became total.

He was into a full, headlong gallop as he hit the defile leading out, so the first of the charging cavalrymen hit him head on.

The heavier-built cavalry horse smashed Jubal's pinto back on its haunches, hurling it against the rocky wall. The sergeant leading the charge was thrown down as his own mount tumbled over, but he swung back into the saddle in more or less the same movement. Jubal was less fortunate. Rock crashed hard against his back as his pony went down and the hammering thunder of the charge blended with the ringing in his ears. He heard the pinto scream as the cavalry horses ploughed it down into the earth, and he rolled against the stone of the defile in a desperate attempt to stay out from under the hooves.

Somehow he succeeded, staggering to his feet as the tail end passed him. He ducked a swinging sabre and ran back the way he had come.

He was in time to see the cavalrymen deploy in tidy formation around the camp. Sabres glinted bright and deadly in the sunlight, falling swift and clean, coming up stained with red. He saw Claw empty a Winchester at the charging soldiers, then run – until he turned, sudden and mean, on the leading trooper. The man screamed as the hook that was Claw's left hand sank deep into his thigh and he felt himself lifted out of the saddle. Then he stopped as the wicked appendage ripped through his throat.

A second trooper, slashing his sabre down at the old, crippled Indian who had killed his buddy, was surprised to find the old man's hook sunk through his cheek. He was hauled backwards off his horse, so his belly was exposed to the knife in Claw's good hand.

He was screaming at the pain of his slit stomach until Claw's body fell across his mouth, spine bared by the savage, down-swinging cut of another rider.

Jubal watched the old chief stagger back onto his feet, waving hook-hand and knife in primeval defiance. Saw him parry a sabre stroke, tumble back as a horse hit him full in the chest, climb to his feet, take a cut that separated his nose from his face, and then die as another sword divided his chest into two sections.

As he watched, Jubal became aware of the solitary Apache levering a Winchester from his prone position off to one side of the canyon's entrance road. Twisted over onto his stomach, the rough splints Jubal had set on his legs, Natchez was picking off the soldiers charging through the rancheria.

Somehow the young war-chief had been overlooked by the attacking cavalry and was lying sprawled behind a boulder, his splinted legs rigid behind him, shooting down the white attackers as they stampeded through the camp.

Jubal didn't stop to think as he veered over towards Natchez. He had only two vague aims, both obscured by the gunsmoke and death all around him; one was to save Natchez, the other to stop the carnage. How he would achieve either objective, he neither knew nor cared, he was operating on pure reflex action, mindlessly, intent only on the immediacy of the moment.

Blindly, uncaring for his own safety, he powered himself across the killing ground in a suicidal run. It took him directly across the path of a sabre-waving trooper in full gallop, quartering the area for fresh targets. The first he saw was Jubal and he came down on the running figure like one of the four horsemen of the apocalypse. Jubal heard a high-pitched yell and turned just in time to see the sun-glinting blade swinging down at his neck, the blue-honed edge dripping scarlet evidence of the trooper's previous trophies.

He didn't stop to worry about which side he was on, or

where the right and wrong of the affair lay. Instead he ducked instinctively under the downswing of the blade, his hands coming up to grab the horse's bridle, so that he was carried along as the trooper swung his blade uselessly around the animal's nose. Then, in an abrupt, somersaulting movement, Jubal's weight brought the animal down to the ground, its head ploughing a long furrow in the sand as it vaulted withers over neck in a pitching fall that catapulted its rider high and fast through the empty air ahead.

The sabre the trooper had been waving at Jubal spun in a glistening arc from his hand as he hit the ground, lifted up for a moment and then slumped unconscious as his big bay horse raced crazily past him where he lay on the shell-pocked sand.

Jubal ignored him, running hard for Natchez' position. He reached it in a wild dive that carried him up and over the young Apache's defensive position, smashing the rifle from his hands as Natchez bellowed an angry cry of protest. Jubal ignored that, too, slapping the barrel aside before Natchez could bring it up again to bear on his torso.

'Dammit,' he snarled, 'don't you know when someone's trying to save your life?'

It looked like Natchez didn't, because he did his best to push Jubal off, ignoring the pain in his legs as he struggled to rejoin the fight. Around him his people were dying, falling beneath the slashing sabres and stuttering handguns of the cavalrymen. Jubal ended his anguish with a right-handed blow that smashed his fist hard against the point of Natchez' chin, snapping the young warrior's head back as his eyes glazed and went blank. He collapsed onto the litter and Jubal yanked the Winchester from his unfeeling grasp.

Holding the gun in one hand and Natchez' shirt in the other, Jubal hauled him back against the wall of the canyon where it was harder for the troopers to spot him.

Crouching protectively beside the Apache, Jubal watched the final demise of Claw's band. Most of the Indians were dead, killed either by the falling howitzer shells or the thundering horsemen. The survivors staggered, dazed, around the camp, herded like human cattle by the blue-clad soldiers. They were pushed slowly into a central group, standing dejected and lost amongst the ruins of their rancheria: the Salt River raiders were finished.

91

Jubal stood up as a youthful captain walked his horse towards him, a long-barrelled Colt held steadily on his chest.

'Who the hell are you, mister?' The soldier was obviously disturbed at the presence of a white man in the camp.

'The name's Cade,' answered Jubal watching the gun. 'Jubal Cade.'

'Jubal Cade?' The captain's reply was unbelieving. 'We came up here because Jubal Cade was taken by the renegades.'

'Yeah, I know,' interrupted Jubal, anxious to establish his credentials, 'Nolan told you. Asked you to come looking for me.'

'That's right.' Doubt sounded in the officer's voice. 'Nolan figgered you for dead an' wanted us to clear out the hostiles. Reckon we done that all right.'

He sounded proud of his work.

'Reckon you did,' Jubal agreed, his eyes scanning the tumbled, broken bodies sprawled around the canyon. 'You cleared them out pretty well.'

'Yeah.' The youngster was holstering his Colt now. 'An' you're Cade, eh?'

'I'm Cade,' Jubal agreed wearily, 'and I'm alive. Thanks to him.' He pointed to the unconscious Natchez.

The soldier looked surprised and Jubal launched one more time into the story of his capture and subsequent release. When he had finished the cavalryman shook his head in wonder.

'Should count in his favour, I guess, but he'll still go to the White Mountain Agency.'

'He might have reservations about that,' grunted Jubal.

He left the officer, proud at having completed his mission, to supervise the exodus of Claw's ravaged band and set about finding his horse. By the time he had caught the nervous animal the Apaches were being driven out of the canyon.

The survivors shuffled through the narrow entrance clutching the few belongings they had managed to salvage, looking a long way removed from the proud, fierce raiders Jubal had gone up against. He sat the pony, watching the ragged column move out, jubilant cavalrymen guarding the flanks. Natchez sprawled dejectedly on a travois pulled along by one of the few remaining mustangs. Whatever they had done in their raids along the Salt River it seemed a tragic way for a proud people to go down and Jubal could not help feeling sympathy for the beaten Indians.

He rode the pinto alongside Natchez and dismounted, waiting for the war chief to open his eyes. When he did, Jubal saw a great sadness.

'Brother,' said Natchez quietly, 'why did you not let me die in battle? The way a warrior should.'

'There's been too much death already,' Jubal answered, 'and sometimes it's a whole lot harder to live. Believe me, I know.'

'What do we have to live for, now?' Natchez demanded. 'A reservation? Prison?'

'Your people will need a leader now that your father is dead,' retorted Jubal.

'A leader? Who needs a leader on the journey to starvation?' Natchez asked bitterly. 'That path a man can find for himself.'

'They're not sending you to the old reservation,' replied Jubal. 'You're headed for the White Mountain Agency. I hear it's not that bad. They got Quakers running the place. You can learn to grow crops. Oats or something.'

Natchez didn't answer.

# CHAPTER FOURTEEN

There was nothing more Jubal could do for the Apaches, so he quit the slow-moving column and headed for the Salt River settlement. The Army was taking the captive hostiles to Cairo by a different route, one that would avoid the mining town; having won his skirmish, the officer in charge had no wish to see the helpless Indians slaughtered by vengeful miners. Instead, he chose the longer trail back to his base, the rail depot and, ultimately, the White Mountain reservation.

Before long the tribe had faded away into the dusty afternoon of the Sierra Mogallon; one more marker pulled from an Army map, one more part of an Indian nation consigned to the history books and forgetfulness.

Jubal, riding slowly down the trail, had his own worries. Andy Prescott, to be exact. The boy was still in the St. Louis clinic and now Jubal had a grubstake that bettered three thousand dollars, he reckoned it was time to go back and check progress. Agnew would still be after his head, of course, but he figured on delivering the money and riding out again pretty fast. Hopefully before the rancher could call down his gunslicks. Either way, the boy represented Jubal's last remaining tie with his old life and the only person he had any real feelings about. He wanted to see Andy again – even though the boy could not see him – no matter what the dangers.

'So,' he thought, 'I draw the mining money out of the bank, pick up whatever Nolan owes me and head for St. Louis.'

The very thought of a comfortable sleeping berth on the Atchison-Topeka was a lure in itself. It seemed like one hell of a long time since he had slept on anything better than a plank bunk with coarse sheets and only a thin blanket between his back and the rough wood.

Yes, he mused, a sleeper, a car with a tub and plenty of hot water, a restaurant wagon. It sounded good.

By the time he reached the mining camp he was feeling pretty cheerful at the prospect of the journey. It was a feeling that faded fast.

The first inkling of something wrong came from the smoke drifting too high into the sky to be the usual cooking fires. The next, from the bodies he saw sprawled in the clumsy attitudes of violent death. They littered mainstreet like confetti after a wedding, except that the wind blowing down the valley left them where they had fallen, very still and very dead.

The chandler's at the approach end of the street was a smoking ruin, the stable next to it still burned, the handful of men trying to douse the blaze too intent on their work to notice Jubal passing. Farther along, a group of half-dressed whores displayed garter belts and black stockings in an incongruous dance as they ran for water to pour against the burning frontage of their tarred-wood bawdy house. The bank seemed relatively intact; until Jubal saw the gaping door and the corpse of a teller sprawled outside. The corpse still clutched the double-action revolver he had tried to use in defence of other people's money; the gaping hole in his back showed that a revolver used by an amateur is no match for a shotgun in the hands of an expert.

Jubal cursed and kicked the pinto into a hard gallop for Nolan's saloon.

The Golden Nugget had suffered like the rest of the town. Its canvas roof was gone, the stink of burning and the crackle of bursting bottles providing an epitaph to Nolan's investment. The owner stood outside, his customary black suit as grey as Jubal's under its coating of ash. Even his thick black hair was greyed by the detritus of the fire. He held a Colt in one hand and a whiskey bottle in the other.

Jubal reined in close to Nolan, who spun around fast and menacing, the Colt lifting in anticipation.

'Fred!' Jubal shouted, conscious of the man's thumb dragging back the hammer. 'Don't you know me?'

'Oh yeah,' Nolan nodded, slowly dropping the hammer, 'I know you. Jubal Cade. The man who went after the renegades on his own. The Army clear out your 'pache friends?' He paused to take a long pull on the bottle. 'They sure as hell didn't clear out the white scum that rode with 'em.'

He shook his head in disbelief, staring first at Jubal, then back at the smouldering ruins of his saloon.

'They came in this morning at sun-up. Seven of them. Would you believe seven men could do this? You better: they did. Fired the town on the first run through and shot anything that moved. Then they came back and shot anything that was still moving. Hit the bank and lifted every last damn' cent anyone had in there.'

He took another long swallow.

'After that they robbed a few places. Only the ones with the money. Like mine. And with the fires an' everythin' there wasn't a sweet goddam anyone could do to stop them. I tried. Got a bullet in my shoulder for the trouble.'

He tossed the whiskey to Jubal.

'Here. Take a drink to your success. You sure as hell fixed the injuns. If you hadn't we wouldn't have had all this.'

For the first time, Jubal became aware of the dark stain showing through the black broadcloth of the gambler's jacket and moved to check the wound.

Nolan backed away.

'No thanks, *doctor*,' he emphasized the word, 'seems to me your brand of medicine's too drastic.'

Jubal recognized the high-pitched note of hysteria in the man's voice and played cautious. He took a swift sip from the bottle and threw it back to Nolan.

'All right, Fred.' He kept his voice as calm and even as possible, conscious of the gun wavering in Nolan's hand. 'So Kincaid and his men hit town because I bust up their deal with the Indians. Don't forget you put me in charge of the militia for just that reason. It was no fault of mine they took it out on you.'

He stopped speaking when Nolan's Colt swung up to level on his belly, hammer pulled back to full cock.

'Shut your fuckin' mouth,' snarled Nolan, 'and look there.' He pointed with the bottle. 'That was Harry. Remember Harry? Best damn' barkeep this side of the Missouri. I never told you, did I? Harry was my brother.'

Jubal followed the pointing bottle, looking towards the front of the burned-out saloon. In amongst the charred wood and blackened glass he made out the shape of a man, what little was left after the flames had died down. The blackened skull, white teeth shining where the lips had burnt away, made him gag. Suddenly he knew why Nolan was half-drunk, half-demented. Equally he knew why Nolan intended to kill him and his hand moved instinctively towards the Colt in its

96

shoulder holster.

'Oh, no,' Nolan smiled like a rabid wolf, 'don't try that. You move for the gun an' I'll blow your knee apart. Then I'll shoot the other. After that, your elbows. Then I'll put a slug in your balls and watch you die.'

Jubal stood still.

'That's better,' grinned Nolan, 'now turn around an' put your hands on the saddle. Away from the rifle. I'm gonna take that gun out of the fancy shoulder-rig an' shoot your arse off if you move while I'm doin' it. After that I'll hang you.'

Jubal turned slowly and placed his hands on the cantle and pommel of the saddle. He took a firm grip and hoped that the pinto wouldn't move suddenly. It didn't, so he had the chance to brace both feet solidly on the ashy ground.

Behind him, Nolan hurled the whiskey bottle into the wreckage of the Golden Nugget and shouted down the street.

'I got him! Come on, fellers, it's lynch time!'

Over the saddle, Jubal could see a group of men break off from salvaging what was left of the townstead and begin to march purposefully in his direction. It didn't seem to matter that he had been asked to hunt out the renegades: the miners needed a donkey in which to stick the tail-end of their blame, no matter how blindly. He was set up as the donkey.

He stood quietly, looking at the length of hemp one miner was carrying over his shoulder, his hands working busily at the hanging knot he was fashioning in the loop at the end.

There were, Jubal decided, two straight choices open to him. He could wait, docile, for death at the hands of a lynch mob; or risk a bullet through his spine in an attempt to get away.

He chose the latter course.

Waiting until he felt Nolan's left hand reaching around his chest to draw the Colt from under his jacket, he pivoted on his right foot, lashing out with his left arm. At the same time, he swung his whole body round against Nolan's right arm. For a moment, the saloon owner's gunhand was pinned against the horse, held there by the weight of Jubal's body. Then the pinto stepped sideways as Jubal's elbow crashed against Nolan's neck.

The blow and the abrupt reversal of his balance sent Nolan crashing to the ground. Jubal fell backwards on top of him, heard Nolan's grunted curse and the ear-splitting blast of the Colt close against his head.

The bullet scorched his hair and whistled on, nicking the underbelly of the pony. Spooked and angry, the pinto did its best to stamp the life out of the men struggling beneath its hooves. One came down on Nolan's gun hand, so that he screamed as his fingers were crushed and rolled away, leaving the bloodstained Colt in the dust.

Jubal rolled, too, moving out from under the deadly hooves. Up the street, the lynch mob was closing fast and he wondered if his desperate gambit would prove successful. He spun to his feet, ignoring Nolan as the crippled gambler moaned, clutching his shattered hand in the ashes of his ruined saloon. Jubal reached over to the Spencer hung to the right of the saddle, hauled the converted repeater from the scabbard, and sent a bullet winging close over the heads of the approaching miners.

It stopped them for a moment before an angry rumbling from the men at the back of the pack drove those at the front on down the street. Jubal realized there was no chance of cowing them with the rifle, so he picked another tactic.

With a sudden yank, he hauled Nolan to his feet and spun the man around to face the crowd. Pressing the muzzle of the Spencer against the gambler's ribs, he shouted at the lynch mob.

'OK! You want to see Fred die?'

They slowed their forward movement.

'You keep on coming and he's dead. Some of you, too.'

The crowd halted for a moment, then two of the braver – or more foolish – miners stepped forward. Jubal shifted the rifle from Nolan's ribs to point at the advancing men. It was difficult firing the long-barrelled gun from the hip, but he had practised long enough to be far more accurate than most. His first shot blasted through the ankle of the leading miner, smashing bone and muscle so that the man fell screaming in front of his followers, before it ricochetted upwards into the thigh of another.

Jubal levered and cocked the rifle one-handed and fired again. The second miner, the one carrying the lynch rope, squealed like a stallion at gelding time as the .30 bullet ripped away his hopes of a happy marriage. Clutching the sudden flowering of blood that covered the front of his levis, he collapsed into the dust.

He lay there squirming as his high-pitched screams stopped the rest of the lynching party more surely than a solid barricade.

Jubal dropped Nolan for a moment, so that he could more easily reload the rifle, then he jerked the man back onto his feet and began to ease down the street. He had seen a horse tethered farther down and he made for it, holding Nolan's collar and the rein of the pinto in his left hand. His right still held the Spencer pointed at the miners.

They were less eager now to pursue him. One was still screaming, high and anguished, while two more were moaning noisily. Jubal took full advantage of their confusion to get to the second horse.

When he reached the animal he pushed Nolan up into the saddle and took off at a fast gallop, leading Nolan behind him like a broken puppet. The man was still trying to clutch his smashed hand in between grabbing for the saddle and Jubal hoped he would stay on the pony: he wanted the shield of Nolan's body between him and the miners.

He had it until he was well out of town and pushing up the steep trail that led away from the ill-fated Salt River camp in the direction of San Rafael.

Near the head of the trail Nolan fell off the horse and Jubal pulled both animals to a stop. He dismounted and walked back to the man who had once been his friend. Nolan was moaning and clutching his hand, staring blindly at the blackened, distorted fingers.

'Fuck you, Jubal,' he muttered as Jubal bent over to examine the extent of his injuries, 'how the hell will I ever handle cards again?'

'You dealt the hand, Fred,' Jubal muttered as he straightened the broken bones, ignoring the whimpering sound of pain that broke from Nolan's lips as he re-arranged torn ligaments and splintered metacarpals, 'if someone clamps down on it, you shouldn't cry over the lost chips.'

Nolan tried to roll away, but Jubal set his knees firmly on the man's shoulders, holding him still until he had finished. Nolan stared blankly at the bandages holding his broken hand together, then up at Jubal.

'Thanks,' he said, and then spat in Jubal's face, 'but I ain't forgotten Harry.'

Jubal contemplated reasoning with Nolan, but decided against it. There was no way of telling when the miners back down the valley trail might gather themselves together enough to organize a posse, and he wanted to be long gone before they even had the chance. He wiped the spittle off his cheek and dragged Nolan back onto his feet.

'Come on, Fred, let's move.'

Nolan put up only a token resistance before he allowed Jubal to push him into the saddle. The day's events seemed to have broken him, mentally first, but later physically. In any event, he let Jubal take up the rein without protesting and followed meekly after the pinto.

Jubal pushed on as fast as he could through the waning light, then used the moon to steer by until he was sure they had a sound lead on any pursuit. He kept riding until his eyelids were getting heavy and the ground ahead of him began to sway and waver in the pale moonlight. At last he stopped, climbing thankfully out of the saddle, and walked back to haul Nolan down.

The saloon owner had fallen asleep as he rode and before he came back awake, Jubal had lashed his wrists and ankles together. He threw a blanket over the man and then settled down to sleep himself. Once again it was a fireless camp and, although he was close to exhaustion and unfeeling of the bitter cold, Jubal was woken by the numbing stiffness in his bones as the sun rose. Nolan, at least, had the comfort of the whiskey he had drunk to keep him insulated; all Jubal could do was slap himself and stamp around in an attempt to get warm that only partially succeeded.

Come noon, both men were as warm as they ever wanted to be. The year was approaching high summer and the upper reaches of the Sierra Mogallon were turning into something that approached close to a furnace under the intensity of the sun.

The big yellow disc hung heavy in the sky, baking the land around them to a uniform shade of greyish yellow. Dust stung their eyes and lips as they rode on, clogged their nostrils and blocked their ears. They carried only the food and water that had been originally stashed on the two horses, so that Jubal was forced to ration both in increasingly sparing quantities.

By the time they had ridden two days out from the Salt River he was seriously worried about Nolan. The man, usually perky, had slipped away into a dumb silence, his eyes glazed over and his lips moving silently. Jubal tried to talk to him, to reason with him, endeavouring to explain the events of his hunt for the renegades and the inevitability of the final outcome. But the loss of his quiet brother seemed to have unhinged Nolan completely and Jubal could no more get through to him than he could find water in the wilderness they traversed.

Indeed, the only mumbled comment Nolan would make was that Kincaid and his men had taken the San Rafael trail. That alone was sufficient to firm Jubal's purpose and keep him heading doggedly in the direction of the town he had left so many weeks before.

And then, he mused, it had been with the prospect of a posse after his blood.

None the less, if Kincaid was headed for San Rafael, that was where he would go, too. He had gotten too close to Mary's killer to give up the chase now. If it meant taking on a vengeful town, then that was what he would do. His only regret was that he had to drag Nolan along with him. The man was a hindrance; he had to be tied up each night to prevent him from attacking Jubal and during the day it became necessary to lash him onto his saddle to stop him from tumbling off as he swayed, vaguely muttering into the parched air. Food and water that might well have sustained one man along the trail had to be shared, but Jubal knew he could not let Nolan go. The gambler had helped him in the past and now, even though he was clearly mad, Jubal felt a debt was owed.

He was not sure how he would do it, or what would happen when he arrived, but he was determined to bring Nolan safely to San Rafael.

His coat collar turned up against the wind that blasted sand like shotgun pellets against his face, and a bandanna tied over his mouth, he pushed on across the back of the Mogallons.

Their going was slow, thanks to Nolan; much slower than Jubal's arrival in the Salt River territory, and after five days, the food ran out. By that time, Jubal had been eking out the water by mixing it with cactus juice, but after one more day the last of the water was gone, too, and they had nothing but the tall cacti to rely on. They used that for two more days before San Rafael showed, distorted and misty as Nolan's mind in the shimmering heat haze.

Lonesome, dirty and dangerous, it looked like paradise on earth to Jubal and he headed for it as fast as his dying pony would take him.

San Rafael greeted the two men with lonesome silence. If anything, it looked even emptier than the last time Jubal had ridden in. The loafers were gone from the street and the watching windows felt empty of eyes. There wasn't even a dog on the roadway; only the buzzing flies stayed the same.

Jubal tried to look casual as he lifted the Spencer from its saddle sheath and rested the gun across his hips, moving along the street towards the stable at the far end.

The tow-headed kid he remembered from the last visit was nowhere in sight, but he could hear horses moving around inside the tall building so he pushed through the loose-hung gate that barred the entrance and rode into the odorous gloom. The sharp smell of manured straw was strong in his nostrils, nearly overriding the sweat of ungroomed horses. Bloated flies drifted lazily through the warm, acidic air and from the stalls on either side of the stable, sad-eyed animals watched the two riders.

Something else impinged on Jubal's nostrils, something sweet and sickly that smelt, even in the malodorous stable, alien. It had nothing to do with horse sweat or uncleaned stalls; it was less sharp than the vinegar stink of old manure, yet somehow more offensive. And it seemed to come from the far end of the stable where the shadows were longest and the flies busiest.

Jubal swung out of the saddle, his rifle swinging to cover the barn. Behind him, Nolan sat where he was tied to the saddle, mumbling softly to himself. Jubal caught part of one incoherent sentence.

'I know. I know what it is. I smelt that before.'

The words triggered memories in Jubal's mind. He was already conscious of danger, of something drastically wrong in San Rafael, but the heady, overpowering odour came close to clouding his thoughts, like the faintly remembered images of an old nightmare.

He left Nolan where he was and walked down the stable

wondering where the boy had got to.

At the far end he saw the youngster.

Flies rose in a heavy crowd as Jubal approached, buzzing, half-lazy, half-angry, from the richest pickings they'd had in weeks.

The tow-headed kid was standing against the far wall, held there by the pitchfork stuck through his chest. His body was black with the winged insects gorging themselves on the dried blood coating his torso and abdomen. It looked as though someone had pinned him there and then used his corpse for target practice, blasting bullets into his teen-aged body until it was a bloody travesty of a human being.

Off to one side lay an ancient, single-shot pocket pistol, hammer down on the empty cylinder: testimony to the boy's defence of his stable.

Jubal gagged as he recognized the stink and reached out to pull the long-tined fork from the youngster's chest. The boy fell soggily to the straw-covered floor, sending a great cloud of flies up into the air, so that Jubal backed away, flapping his left hand to keep them from settling on him.

Outside there was still no movement, nothing to suggest watchers; indeed, there was nothing to suggest that San Rafael was anything other than a ghost town.

Cautiously, his nerves taut, muscles ready for instantaneous action, Jubal walked back to Nolan.

'Told you,' muttered the gambler, 'told you I smelled it before. Know that smell.' For a second his eyes cleared and he spoke sanely. 'It was back on the Salt after the renegades hit us. When they killed Harry and the rest. I smelled it then. The smell of death.'

He stopped in a fit of giggling as Jubal turned the horses out of the stable, leading them around the building to the shadowed corral set off to one side. He hauled Nolan clear of the saddle and pushed the man up against one wall of the stable while he doled water into the trough and dragged hay out of the rack.

The town was still quiet as he loosed the stalled horses and drove them into the corral. Then, when he was sure the animals would be all right, he turned back to Nolan.

'OK, Fred, let's take a walk.'

Unprotesting, Nolan followed after Jubal as he walked away

103

from the livery stable. It was a weird sensation to pass by the sun-bleached houses and shopfronts devoid of any sign of life. Even in San Rafael there should have been some kind of movement on the street. Especially now, with the dead boy mute evidence of recent violence. Jubal reckoned he had been killed no more than a day ago and even if every able-bodied man in the place had ridden out after his killers, there should still be women and oldsters around. He braced the Spencer against his hip and kept his thumb on the hammer as he moved down mainstreet.

Warily, he climbed the steps onto the dusty boardwork, hugging the shelter of the buildings as he paced cautiously past the enpty windows.

The first doorway he reached was the entrance to a hardware store. Shovels, hammers, axes and boxes of nails were gathering dust behind grime-smeared glass; the door hung open, letting in the sunlight to illuminate the inside of the store. There was no-one there. The place looked to be in order as Jubal swung inside, moving fast to the wall at his right, the Spencer shifting in a flat arc to cover the room. Rakes and hoes stood in ordered lines down the centre, barrels of screws and tacks flanked the side walls, saddles hung from a rack set against a glass-fronted cabinet displaying handguns and rifles. The glass was broken and the lighter patches on the sun-faded felt backcloth showed where weapons had been removed.

On the floor to the left of the cabinet lay the storekeeper. The back of his skull was a seething canteen for the flies. Five feet above his body, a hole in the wall showed where the bullet had exited, to embed itself in the rough wood. The smell was not so bad as in the stable, but it was still there, cloyingly sweet in the afternoon air.

Jubal didn't bother to check the corpse. He backed out of the store, pulling back the hammer of the Spencer as he went, angling the barrel downwards in readiness for action, and continued the lonely walk down the street.

It looked as though his guess about Kincaid's direction had been right. If renegade Indians had hit the place there would have been more signs of slaughter, fires would have blazed, hair been lifted. What he had seen so far indicated a coldly calculated raid with wanton killing thrown in for the sheer fun of seeing bullets hit a body: San Rafael carried Kincaid's trademark.

The next building was a milliner's. Even a one-horse town like San Rafael contained an element of fashion-conscious ladies, though now they would find it hard to buy their bonnets because the proprietress had sprayed blood over her central display. Wide-brimmed gauze-draped sun-bonnets were smeared with the same dye as the little, peak-fronted poke bonnets that granted her a degree of modesty where she sprawled, legs spread wide beneath an up-pulled skirt. Her cambric pantaloons were torn apart and bloodied like the front of her ripped dress. She must have been pretty enough to rape, but now it was hard to tell, because a bullet had removed most of her face. Jubal left her where she lay and moved on down the street.

He didn't look into any more of the open, empty stores: there were two places where the townsfolk might have gathered, the saloon or the hotel and he headed straight for the closest.

With Nolan still walking silently behind him, he reached the saloon. The small, square-paned windows were too dirty to see through, so he sidled up to the bat-wing doors. He was about to crouch down to peer beneath the wooden slats when Nolan pushed past him, knocking him aside as he shoved through to the interior. Something about the sight or smell of the place must have kindled a memory in the demented mind, drawing the gambler as surely as the blood on the corpses drew the flies.

As Nolan went in Jubal heard a sudden growl of conversation. Whatever had happened in San Rafael, it appeared that the citizens had gathered in the Silver Dollar. Hoping they had forgotten about the killing of their marshal, Jubal followed Nolan's lead.

He was two paces inside, his rifle covering the crowd of men and women seated in a nervous circle in the centre of the long room, when he realized his mistake. The whole scene was far too still, too quiet; the citizens were watching him as though they expected a thunderbolt to strike him down.

The thunderbolt was a familiar voice.

'Cade. Welcome to San Rafael. I figgered you might follow us, so I waited for you.'

The words ended in a bellow of cold laughter that didn't

105

shift the aim of the matched Colts Kincaid was pointing at Jubal's chest. Around the room, sheltered by drapes and pillars, four renegades covered the central area with Winchesters. Up on the balcony that encircled three sides of the saloon, three more outlaws pointed scatterguns down at the crowd.

Jubal's own gun was centred on Kincaid's midriff, the muzzle unwavering as he took up the trigger slack.

'You gonna try it?' Kincaid jeered. 'One shot from that rifle an' we blow the whole damn' place apart. All these good folks'll get to die knowin' it's yore doin'.'

'Maybe.' Jubal could feel hatred drawing the skin tight across his cheekbones. 'But you won't be around to see it. You'll be holding the hole in your guts.'

'Now you could be right,' Kincaid spoke with the flat monotones of total indifference, 'but you'll kill just one man. Maybe. Then you'll die knowin' these people are followin' you. You want that?'

More than life itself, Jubal wanted to squeeze the trigger, see the .30 calibre shell plant a red flower on Kincaid's body. But to do that knowing it meant the death of so many innocent bystanders was something else. Deep-etched though his hatred was, he could not knowingly sentence the others to his own fate.

Kincaid read the confusion in Jubal's eyes and laughed, harsh and grating.

'Yeah. I thought so. You ain't got the stomach for it, have you, Cade?'

Reluctantly, Jubal shook his head.

'All right, set the rifle down. Slow an' easy, so I don't get spooky.'

Gently, Jubal eased the hammer down, then stooped to set the converted carbine on the floor. He stood up slowly as Kincaid shouted to one of the men on the balcony.

'Morgan! Take him upstairs an' keep that shotgun on his back. If he makes a move, pull both triggers.'

The man called Morgan came down the stairs slow and cautious, the twin barrels of the scattergun pointing in Jubal's direction, though at that range it would make little difference where he aimed it. The barrels had been sawn off to little more than nine inches, so that the buckshot would spread in a huge fan of tearing destruction. Jubal stood very still, hoping the outlaws would forget to search him.

Kincaid's pleasure at capturing his long-time enemy seemed to have made him careless; either that, or he was so used to seeing Jubal carrying the Spencer that it did not occur to him that the small, grey-suited man might carry a second gun. Whatever the reason, no-one thought to check beneath Jubal's coat, where the handgun still rested in its shoulder holster. He had not been told to raise his hands, so he kept both arms stretched stiff out from his sides, hiding the bulge beneath his jacket.

Morgan moved around him and prodded the big Remington against the small of his back.

'OK, friend, start walking. Up the stairs to the big sleep.'

Jubal obeyed meekly, his mind working furiously to find some new angle that would permit him to escape. Nothing came and the Remington nestled hard against his back served to emphasize the futility of precipitate action. He allowed Morgan to guide him, like a steer in a slaughterhouse, up the stairs and along the balcony to a room at the end. It was on the corner of the saloon, at the back, and must have been occupied by one of the staff, Jubal guessed. At any rate, there was only a tiny skylight, too small to offer escape, and a brass bed flanked by a washstand.

Morgan used the shotgun to push Jubal inside, pausing as he turned to lock the door.

'Make yoreself comfortable, friend,' he grinned, 'I kinda think yore stay's gonna be a short one. Like they say, there's three steps to heaven an' you can plainly see yore foot's on the first one.'

He didn't hear Jubal's reply, but if he had – and still felt any respect for his mother – he might have pushed Jubal up the other two steps right then.

# CHAPTER FIFTEEN

Locked inside the tiny room with a shotgun guarding the door, Jubal saw little prospect of escape. He didn't know when, or how, Kincaid planned to kill him, but that was the obvious end of the incident. The killer must have led his gang of cutthroats to San Rafael after hitting the mining settlement and decided to lie up there and await any pursuit. Jubal swore at himself for walking into the trap so blindly: he knew Kincaid's style well enough to have guessed the move and should never have allowed his desire for revenge or the lynch mob to push him into what now appeared to be suicidal action.

Still, he shrugged his shoulders in resignation, he was in a firm-sprung trap; now the thing was to find a way out of it.

He examined the room in minute detail, and came up with exactly nothing. It was about nine by nine, most of that taken up by the bed, the wash table and a small closet. One asset was the clean shirt he found inside the cupboard. His own was dust-caked and stained with old blood and he shucked it gratefully, taking time to sluice his sweaty chest with water from the jug. If he was about to die, he mused, at least he would die clean. When he had finished, he pulled on the fresh shirt. It was a perfect fit; but then, he remembered, one of the barkeeps he had seen draped cold and dead over the long pine counter had been about his size.

Feeling a lot better for washing and the change of clothes, he hung the shoulder rig across his back and pulled on his jacket. He still had two aces in his hand: he was alive and he had the Colt. How long either would stay with him, or whether he would get a chance to play them, he did not know, but being alive and armed was a whole lot better than stopping a slug.

He looked up at the skylight, wondering if he was small enough to wriggle through. Thirty seconds of self-persuasion told him he wasn't, but then another thought occurred to him. Did Morgan know that? It was, at best, a slender chance, but it looked like the only one he had.

Cat-silent, he padded over to the door and pressed his ear against the thin wood frame. Outside he could hear Morgan shuffling his feet as he waited for fresh orders, and over that sound the low hum of voices from the room below. It sounded as though the outlaws were debating their next move and, to judge by the raised voices that echoed up to the balcony, arguing over something. Jubal hoped that the discussion was taking up all their attention as he moved back to the centre of the room. He climbed onto the bed, balancing precariously on the soggy springs, and set about prising the skylight open. It was old and rusted into its fastenings, the frame warped by sun and rain, but after several minutes of furtive work, he got it open. Then he stepped back onto the floor and gently shifted the washstand over to the middle of the room. He drew the .30 calibre Colt and shoved it under a pillow to deaden the sound of the hammer cocking, then he stepped back and measured the distance between table and door frame.

He stood back, waiting until the voices below rose again, then kicked the table over. As it fell, the jug and wash bowl crashing noisily to the floor, he jumped over to stand behind the door.

Morgan came through fast, the shotgun extended before him, jerking up to cover the open skylight as he cursed the apparent escape.

He stopped when the muzzle of Jubal's Colt pressed against his skull, just behind his left ear.

'Keep your mouth shut and your finger off the trigger,' Jubal murmured, 'that way you might live a while longer.'

Morgan froze up like a chicken with a diamondback under its beak. His fingers lifted off the double triggers of the Remington and he allowed Jubal to take the heavy gun out of his hand. Carefully, Jubal eased the hammers down and set the gun on the floor behind him.

'Get onto the bed. Face down.' He prompted Morgan with the barrel of the Colt.

The outlaw obeyed without protest, fear-sweat standing cold on his face. He stretched on the bed, a nervous tic jerking the skin of his jaw, his knuckles showing white where he grasped the rails of the bedhead. He was unable to still the trembling in his legs, his boots drumming a soundless tattoo against the grubby sheets.

'Oh dear God,' he mumbled against the stained pillow, 'don't let him kill me. Please. Please. God, don't let him. Don't let him kill me, God.'

His prayer went unanswered. Jubal lowered the hammer of the Colt and shifted the big gun in his fist, moving his finger off the trigger. Holding it so that the hammer was shut down against accidental discharge, he smashed the butt against Morgan's neck. The outlaw grunted into the pillow, his head snapping back against the impact. Carefully, with surgical precision, Jubal hit him again, driving the edge of the heavy wooden butt hard between the delicate vertebrae holding Morgan's head on his shoulders. He felt the shock of breaking bone vibrate up through the gun and saw bright red blood spout from the outlaw's mouth as shards of spinal cortex punctured his throat. Deliberately, Jubal hit him twice more, so that Morgan's head twisted around, hanging at a crazy angle as a livid bruise spread across the tan of his broken neck. He made no sound, dying with his mouth pressed hard against the pillow while outside his fellow renegades continued to argue.

Jubal stepped back, holstering the Colt and picking up the scattergun. Quickly he checked the dead man for extra cartridges, coming up with three more loads for both barrels. He shoved them into his pockets and cat-footed through the doorway.

Below him as he crouched on the balcony he could see Kincaid arguing with his men. The balcony guards had gone down to join the others spread around the saloon and it looked as though at least three retained principles of some kind because they were trying to talk Kincaid out of opening fire on the prisoners. Kincaid, Jubal gathered, was backed by three more of the remaining six renegades in his desire to slaughter everyone.

For a moment, he contemplated ending the discussion by the simple expedient of emptying both barrels of the Remington into Kincaid's back. But he knew the spreading shot would hit too many of the innocents along with the scarfaced man, so he opted for a more subtle diversion.

He paced silently along the balcony to one of the kerosene lanterns hung in an alcove on the wall. Then, cradling the shotgun in his arms, he fumbled matches from a vest pocket and lit the lamp. It was a copper-bottomed affair with a glass funnel containing the wick, and it was full. Jubal turned the wick up to its full extent, waited until the blue-gold flame had a firm grip, and then tossed the lantern out over the crowd.

It hit the bar, where puddles of cheap whiskey washed around the bodies of the dead bartenders, and shattered in a spreading pool of flame. The whiskey ignited more slowly and Jubal wondered just what had gone into it as the renegades turned in surprise towards the blaze spreading rapidly along the dry planking. Women began to scream as the flames ate into the old wood and Kincaid turned, glaring up at the balcony. Before he could aim accurately, Jubal was gone, darting towards a window at the back of the saloon. Kincaid's bullets ricochetted uselessly off the upper woodwork, blasting splinters from where Jubal had been standing.

The window was set solid into its frame and Jubal had to stop long enough to pick up a chair and hurl it through the glass before he could effect his escape.

It was enough time for one of Kincaid's men to hit the stairs up to the balcony, triggering his Winchester as he came.

Billy-Joe was a Kentucky boy, raised in the bluegrass country where kids learned to ride and shoot as soon as they were old enough to stand. He had used a rifle since before he knew when and reckoned himself the finest shot in Kincaid's bunch. He had thrown in with the scarfaced man two years ago, finding the life of outlawry a whole lot more exciting than raising horses on his old man's spread. It wasn't easy all the time, they slept cold and lonesome too often for Billy-Joe's liking, but the good times were real good: they gave him full vent to express his inborn love of killing. He had backed Kincaid in wanting to wipe out the whole of San Rafael and now he was angry at the interruption.

He came up the stairs fast and mad, levering the Winchester to put down a field of fire that would confuse the awkward little bastard they had planned to kill later on, nice and slow so they could listen to him squeal.

Billy-Joe was too confident of his own prowess with a rifle to contemplate anything other than shooting the prisoner stone cold dead. That was why he came up over the head of the stairs at a run, firing the rifle on the way. Unfortunately for Billy-Joe the awkward little bastard had other ideas about his future and they were entirely contradictory.

111

Jubal heard the chair crash through the window at the same time he herad boot-heels thundering up the stairs, accompanied by a crescendo of rifle fire. He swung around, dropping to a crouch as he pointed the Remington at the stair-well.

Billy-Joe came up over the head at a dead run and went back the same way, only as his unfeeling feet paced down the wooden steps he wasn't firing the Winchester any more. He couldn't see anything and his hands didn't seem to work properly since that big red flame had sprouted out in front of his face. He couldn't figure out what had happened to him, but somehow his upper body had gone numb and his face felt like it had been rubbed hard down into a sand-pit. There was an odd salty taste in his mouth and his tongue hurt when he touched it to the ragged edges of his shattered teeth.

Something had gone horribly wrong, but exactly what it was, Billy-Joe couldn't work out. So he kept pacing backwards down the stairs, shaking his head as he went and wondering why he felt so sick all of a sudden.

He opened his mouth and vomited without stopping his backward walk to wonder why the woman down below was screaming at the stream of frothy blood spewing from his lips.

Mrs. Danvers was screaming at the sight of a walking corpse backing slowly down the stairs of a burning saloon. She had seen people die before, but always in bed and tidily. She had never seen a man with an ounce of heavy-gauge pellets in his face and torso spitting blood all over his trousers as he shook his head and tried to see out of eyes that weren't there anymore.

Billy-Joe kept listening to her as he completed his slow descent, but when he turned at the foot of the stairs he lost his direction in the wail that went up from the other women.

He stood for a long moment, turning his head from side to side so they could all see the white bone of his cranium, showing through where the ought-ought pellets had torn away his hair, the red holes that had been his eye sockets peering sightlessly out from the pocked remains of his face. He tried to say something, but no-one understood because his lower jaw was hanging by a single tendon down against his chest. He gave up on the attempt and fell backwards, hitting the floor with a thud that sent a rain of blood up out of the holes in his chest.

As he died, Billy-Joe wondered why he didn't feel anything

and why he could see only a red mist. Then, very briefly, he wondered why he had not stayed to raise horses with his father. Everyone said that old E. A. Stuart raised the finest horses they'd ever seen; maybe it would have been a better life.

Jubal didn't wait to see the boy die. He had triggered the scattergun without thinking and then followed the chair through the broken window in a shallow dive that he hoped would land him someplace reasonably soft.

Clutching the Remington in one hand and protecting his face with the other, he powered through the window. Outside, the roof of an outlying shack stopped his fall. He hit the clinker-built construction and rolled over, tumbling down off the building so that he landed feet-first in the dust back of the saloon. A quick check told him he hadn't broken anything and he ran over to a small hut opposite the larger structure.

As he reached the flimsy building he heard a shout from behind him and threw himself headlong through the doorway. Rolling with the fall, he came back over facing out in time to see two of Kincaid's men emerging from the rear of the saloon. Behind them he could see flames climbing the walls of the wooden building and hear screaming from inside. Then the sound was shut off under the thunder of the Remington.

The leading outlaw went back like a kite caught in a sudden downdrop of wind, fluttering his arms as his handgun spun away from his deadened fingers, a checkerboard of red appearing across the front of his shirt. He cannoned against the second man, who yelled as the buckshot ploughed furrows of crimson over his face. Incensed by the pain, he pushed the body of his companion to one side and triggered two fast shots at Jubal's position. Jubal, however, had twisted off to one side of the shack, pushing a fresh load into the shotgun.

The outlaw's bullets threw splinters up from the wood floor as the man hurled himself in Jubal's direction. He fired as he ran, coming through the doorway with only one shell left in the chamber of his Colt. As he crossed the threshold, Jubal snapped the Remington closed and swung it up without cocking. The heavy barrels caught the renegade under the chin, stopping him dead in his tracks as reflex action blasted his last shot uselessly against the tar-paper roof. He stood for a second, numbed by the blow, then hurtled back the way he had

113

come when Jubal fired the shotgun. It was pressed up against the man's ribs so that the discharge tore him apart, sending the upper half of his body in a high arc against the rear door of the saloon as his abdomen and legs fell like cut trees into the dust of the alley.

Jubal powered to his feet and ran out of the hut, loading the shotgun as he went.

He ignored the building that was now blazing behind him, intent only on finding a vantage point from which he could pick off the remaining four outlaws. The confusion of the fire might not do the saloon any good, but it couldn't harm the hostages' chances of escape. And Jubal anticipated using that confusion to his own advantage.

As he ran, he wondered what had become of Nolan. The gambler's madness had seemed to protect him when he entered the saloon, as though the blank glaze over his own eyes clouded the vision of others, and Jubal had seen him shoved across to join the rest of the prisoners without any special attention being paid to him. Hopefully, it would stay that way, though at that moment Jubal had more immediate concerns. Like staying alive.

Kincaid still had three men to back him and there was no telling which way the townspeople would jump if they remembered Jubal as the killer of Longridge.

Fear and fire, he reckoned, would keep the citizens of San Rafael occupied long enough for him to settle the score with Mary's killer -- or die trying -- and get out of town. If it was in front of a posse, then too bad. The cards fell the way they were dealt and all a man could do was pick up his hand and play it as best he could.

He swung around a corner that would lead him out onto the main drag and heard the vicious crack of a Winchester. The bullet hit the wall at his back, blasting chunks of creosote into the air. Jubal fired the Remington as he threw himself to the ground, but at that range the sawn-off barrels were useless, spreading pellets in so wide a pattern that none found a target. Kincaid's man laughed and levered the rifle for a second shot as Jubal dropped the shotgun and hauled the Colt from underneath his jacket.

He came up on one knee, cradling the pistol in both hands for the long shot across the street as the outlaw squeezed off his second round. Fired fast, the bullet missed Jubal by several inches so that he had time to sight and squeeze as the Winchester's lever was pumping down and then up again. His training told in the way his first shot took the renegade exactly where he had aimed it: dead centre of the chest. The man took three steps backwards, dropping the rifle as his hands came up to clutch the sudden pain in his breastbone. Jubal fired once more, the .30 calibre bullet ramming the man's belt buckle through his shirt into his stomach. Bullet and buckle embedded themselves in his gut, doubling him over as his intestines tangled round his feet in a yellow and red explosion of gore. He dropped his hands away from the hole in his chest and collapsed, trying hard to hold on to his spilling insides. As Jubal picked up the scattergun and ran towards the head of mainstreet, Kincaid's third man died.

Jubal reached the entrance of the Silver Dollar as a crowd of panic-stricken citizens charged out. The flames had a firm hold by now, licking up the outside of the building to catch the tar-paper and creosote walls of the stores to either side, and as he had guessed, the conflagration afforded him the advantage of complete confusion. He shouldered his way through the yelling people, using them as a shield between him and Kincaid's men. In the chaos, he took the chance of darting inside the saloon to grab his Spencer, still resting against the front wall where he had first placed it. He hefted the familiar weight in both hands, grateful to have got back his favourite weapon, leaving the shotgun on the floor of the burning saloon.

Then he darted back to the street. No-one spotted him as he ran towards the livery stable; like the inhabitants of the nameless mining town, the people of San Rafael were fighting a losing battle against the fire that was consuming their homes.

The buildings were mostly wooden and dried by long years in the New Mexican sun. Additionally, they were nearly all covered with highly inflammable creosote or tar-paper, so that the slightest spark took easy hold, growing into a flaming pyre of red destruction as the late-afternoon breeze fanned avid life into the licking flames.

Smoke roiled through the warm air, lying heavily over the confusion as Jubal slipped wraith-like up mainstreet. He had no intention of leaving San Rafael until Kincaid was dead, but before he faced the scarred man, he needed fresh ammunition,

115

and for that he had to get to his horse. He was halfway there before anyone spotted him. Then a wild cry echoed through the smoke.

'Cade! Jubal Cade! You can't get away.'

He recognized Nolan's voice and part-turned as the black-clad figure came running out of the fires. Like some demented demon, Nolan hurled himself straight at Jubal, arms spread wide in a madman's embrace. Jubal swung the stock of the Spencer in a short arc that knocked Nolan off into the dust of mainstreet and kept on running. But Nolan was oblivious to the pain; he fell, rolled, and came back on his feet in one continuous movement, starting doggedly after his quarry the moment he was upright again.

Behind him, others had heard the yell and started on their own pursuit.

Jubal reached the stable about four paces ahead of Nolan and a dozen yards in front of Kincaid and his two remaining men. He vaulted the rail around the stockyard and grabbed the bridle of the pinto, pulling the horse around so that it sheltered him from the fire Kincaid was putting down.

As he dragged a box of cartridges from the saddlebag two bullets hit the horse, one driving deep into its underbelly, the other nicking its spinal column. The animal screamed shrilly as its hindquarters collapsed under the dead weight of its broken back and whinnied blood across the corral from its ruptured stomach.

Jubal paused long enough to end the animal's misery with a .30 rifle bullet, then triggered two fast shots in Kincaid's direction before turning towards the shelter of the stable.

The big building was far enough away from the rest of the town to be safe from the flames, although the acrid smell of burning wood and the roaring sound of flaming timbers were spooking the horses. They milled nervously around the corral, trotting in jumpy circles as they pushed against the fence posts in an effort to find a way out. As Jubal hit the entrance to the stable, bullets peppered the woodwork around him and he realized that Kincaid was planning to box him. He rolled across the straw to the shelter of the door frame and swung the Spencer in the direction of the corral.

The gate was a flimsy affair of crossed poles held in position by ropes and three shots served to cut the cord, opening the corral to the street. The whistling bullets panicked the terrified horses into a wild stampede. As Jubal had hoped, they thundered round the fence until they came to the open gate, then raced through, heading straight for Kincaid and his men. Nolan was bowled head over heels by the leading pony, but the others saw them coming and scattered to either side of the dusty track, seeking shelter from the maddened animals.

The diversion gave Jubal the time he needed to reload the Colt and the Spencer and drag a bale of straw across the entrance. Then he bellied down behind the frail barricade and waited for the siege to begin.

As the stampeded horses disappeared into the smoke Kincaid urged his men on towards the stable. Jubal raked the street with gunfire, laying down a wall of screaming lead that sent the outlaws diving for cover. They returned the fire from behind the protection of doorways and pillars, ploughing bullets through the wide, dark opening of the stable. Jubal dodged from side to side of the straw bale as he replied in kind, but he could find no clear target and his shots either hit woodwork or spanged off up the street.

It was a stalemate situation with both sides pinned down and looking for a fresh gambit.

Nolan provided it. The gambler was spreadeagled in the dust midway between Jubal and Kincaid. No-one had paid him any attention since the horse had knocked him down, but now he began to moan softly, moving his head from side to side as though trying to rid it of a bad ache. He rolled over onto his face and pushed himself up onto hands and knees. Unsteadily, he got to his feet and began to walk slowly towards the stable.

Jubal cursed as the tottering figure blocked his field of fire.

Kincaid saw the advantage and took it fast. He ran from cover, heading diagonally across the street in the direction of a flatbed wagon standing in front of the hardware store. He hollered for his men to join him and they broke cover, moving fast towards the wagon.

By the time Nolan had reached the stable and Jubal was able to drag him down to the temporary safety of the straw bale, the three outlaws were pushing the buggy up the street. They sheltered behind the wooden bulk of the thing, so that Jubal's aim was effectively blocked as it trundled closer to his position. He tried shooting for their legs, aiming under the flatbed, but the iron-hooped wheels deflected his bullets, rico- chetting them away on useless trajectories.

In the stable, Nolan was still shaking his head and looking dazed. Then, abruptly, he turned to Jubal.

'What the hell's goin' on?' His voice was normal.

'Shooting war,' Jubal grunted tersely, 'keep your head down and you might just hang on to it.'

Nolan peered around the bale, studying the blazing town that formed a backdrop to the tableau of the advancing wagon.

'Hell, it looks like the Salt River camp.' He shook his head again, as though to clear foggy thoughts from the corridors of his mind. 'Where are we?'

Jubal risked a quick glance at Nolan, wondering exactly what was going on. 'You don't know?'

'No.' It sounded genuine. 'I feel like I've been on a drunk fer a week. Can't hardly remember anythin' since the Nugget took fire.' He broke off, a stark memory of pain showing in his dark eyes. 'An' Harry died.'

Jubal had read about cases of hysterical amnesia during his training period in England. Broadly, he understood the prin- ciples of the condition: that an acute emotional shock could throw a person's mind out of gear, so that facts, realities, were rejected as a protection against accepting the hard facts of a situation. Once, in London, he had seen a man being treated for the same complaint. He had been sixty years old and his wife had died; the man had simply refused to accept his widowerhood: he maintained that his wife still lived, he talked to her, held back empty chairs so that a mental ghost could seat herself, ladled food onto plates set before an empty place. Society deemed him mad; he lived within his own reality.

The treatments had not been pleasant. Alternating baths of very hot and exceedingly cold water, sudden shocks, the violent shouting of male nurses. The aim had been to push the man's mind forcibly back into the generally accepted reality. Jubal wondered if the collision with the horse had done that for Nolan.

In spite of the situation, he laughed to himself. If his theory was right he could be making medical history; if he lived long enough to tell anyone about it.

'Fred,' he was watching the advancing buggy as he spoke, 'Harry died over a week ago. After Kincaid fired the settlement. You've been kind of sick since then.'

'Guess I musta been,' murmured Nolan thoughtfully. 'Seems I got a notion I tried to kill you aways back. That right?'

'Yeah,' grunted Jubal. The wagon was drawing too close for his liking. 'That's right.'

'Gee,' Nolan sounded honestly contrite, 'I'm sorry. I guess the saloon goin' up an' Harry dying like that kinda threw me.'

'It damn' near threw me, too,' Jubal grinned. He wasn't sure why he was smiling: he couldn't get a clear shot at the three outlaws and in a few minutes they would be pushing that damned buggy in through the doorway. 'You carrying a gun?'

'No, I ain't.' Nolan sounded apologetic. 'Don't think I've had one since the camp burned out.'

A chord was plucked on Jubal's memory.

'Tell me something, Fred,' he handed Nolan his Colt as he was speaking. 'I never did get to ask what that place was called.'

'The settlement?' Nolan sounded surprised. 'Nobody ever got to call it anythin'. It was just a town with no name. Drifter off the High Plains found gold there. Man called Clint – no-one ever did know his last name – started diggin' an' kept coming up with a few dollars more. After that folks got driftin' in, some good, some bad, most ugly. Harry was pretty ugly. That was why people called him Dirty Harry.'

He was checking the Colt as he spoke and when he had finished, he spun around to send two ranging shots at the wagon that was now only a few yards from the stable.

# CHAPTER SIXTEEN

The backboard of the buggy was pock-marked with bullet holes, as scarred as the face of a smallpox victim. The iron-girdled wheels were scraped and glistening where Jubal's shots had hit, but it kept on coming. And from behind its shelter, Kincaid and his two fellow outlaws kept up a fusillade of rifle fire.

As it pushed closer, Jubal and Nolan backed off down the stable. They kept low so that Kincaid wouldn't see them go and when they reached a point midway down the barn, they split to either side and climbed fast up the twin ladders to the loft. Bellied down over the straw-covered slats, they waited for the renegades to come in. Kincaid, though, was too cautious. The wagon stopped at the entrance as a volley of shells pumped through the bale of straw, then a figure broke away and ran back down the street.

A few moments later, he returned, holding an armful of shining copper and glass tubes.

Jubal wondered what the next move would be. It was up to Kincaid, who held the advantage now; all Jubal wanted was a chance to put a bullet into the scarfaced man.

There was a long silence as the outlaws clustered in back of the wagon, then one of the copper tubes glinted in the late afternoon sun as it arced high through the air, musty with floating motes of stable dust, and crashed against a stall. As it hit, flames erupted over the dry wood and Jubal recognized the thing as a kerosene lantern. Four more were pitched in after the first, the liquid contents spreading avidly over straw and woodwork, the bright flames taking instantaneous hold.

The heady stink of burning manure raised tears in Jubal's eyes as smoke clouded his vision. Across the central aisle of the stable, Nolan was coughing badly, invisible behind the rising pall. Below, Kincaid and his men came in fast and murderous.

José Garcia led the charge, levering a Winchester Yellow-boy up at the loft as he ran through the flames. He was the oldest member of the gang, a moustached Mexican who had joined Kincaid four years ago after killing his own brother in a knife fight in Mazatlan. He'd had a good thing going with his brother's wife until Manuel had walked in one warm, September evening and objected to the games going on amid the sweaty sheets.

José had planted a blade in Manuel's ribs and started running. Along the way he traded his peasant's huaraches for high-heeled, hand-tooled boots and his knife for a silver-plated Colt. At the same time he forgot his farming background and teamed up with Kincaid on the owlhoot route.

He remembered the farm for the first time in years as Jubal's bullet hit him between the second and third ribs, exactly where he had stuck the knife into Manuel. He felt his ribs splinter and his life flow away through the hole as images of his white-haired mother and sad-eyed father danced before his closing eyes. Then they were replaced by the smiling face of Manuel, one arm outstretched as though welcoming his errant brother into the afterworld.

José Garcia was suddenly conscious of a foul taste in his mouth and realized that he was lying face down in a pile of horse shit, dying.

'What a lousy, cruddy way to go,' he thought, 'at least you died cleaner, Manuel.'

The blood-stained figure came closer, the hand touching José's arm now. Then the other hand came into view and Manuel smiled as he thrust a long-bladed knife deep between José's ribs.

'How can a ghost kill me?' José wondered. Then he rolled onto his back and died.

Jim-boy Chandler pulled up fast as he saw José go down. The old Mexican had always been impetuous, running into trouble as though he wanted to die, like some old memory was driving him to risk his life as often as he could. Jim-boy was more cautious, he had to be to realize his two great ambitions in life: to become a great gunfighter and enjoy a rich old age. Joining Kincaid's mob had seemed to offer both. Surely, he was rich now; with José dead only two men would share the fifteen thousand dollars they had lifted from that stinking mine-town. And if the two men hiding up in the loft of the burning stable would just come down and face him in a straight gunplay, he was sure he could kill them clean and easy.

Trouble was, they were up top and he was down bottom, with Kincaid shouting for him to move on in and finish them off.

Jim-boy was exactly seventeen years old, a fair-haired, slack-mouthed kid with five notches conscientiously cut into his gun butt. In his own opinion, he was the best thing since John Wesley Hardin, maybe even better. Like his dead buddy, Billy-Joe, he had a natural instinct for the business, he enjoyed watching a man's face as the .44 shell took the life out of his body. Somehow, it seemed to make Jim-boy a bigger man, someone to reckon with: a shootist.

Right now, though, he had to admit he was scared of two things. Kincaid was one, the two men hidden behind the smoke, the other.

One, at least, had a rifle and Jim-boy hoped like hell that the smoke lifting up through the rafters would obscure his aim long enough for him to bring the twin Colts he had adopted since meeting Kincaid into play.

He took a deep breath and ran down the aisle, triggering the handguns at either side of the loft.

He was halfway down and still firing when the roof above him gave way under the blaze. Through the great mass of falling, burning timber came a demonic figure dressed all in black, except where flames licked over clothes and hair. It landed in a heap just a few feet from Jim-boy, who stood gaping and still at the incredible sight.

Nolan came up on his feet without stopping to worry about broken bones. He could feel his hair burning on his scalp, the cloth of his jacket smouldering over his back. He didn't care, he only wanted to gun down the men who had killed Harry.

Crouching like some burning vision from hell, he lifted Jubal's Colt in his right hand. His left swung up and over, the palm hitting the hammer as the finger of his right hand held the trigger back. Five times he fanned the gun, laughing as the .30 calibre shells blew holes in Jim-boy's chest and stomach. He watched the kid thrown backwards by the force of the bullets, walking at first with his own guns dangling unused from useless, frightened fingers, then half-running under the impact, finally toppling into the blazing straw of a burning stall.

As he died, Jim-boy wondered how he could have been so careless as to let a madman gun him down and what folks would say about so sorry an end to a promising career.

Maybe mom had been right, he thought, when she told him not to take his guns to town. He had, though, and now he was dead and the last thing he saw was a burning man running down the stable at Kincaid.

The scarfaced man watched Nolan coming, wondering how in the hell anyone could keep moving with their whole body on fire. Nolan looked like one of those life-size puppets the Mexicans lit up at fiestas; his coat was blazing, sending clouds of fire up around his burning hair, the hand holding the gun was blistering red as the sleeve of his jacket burned, his face was a hideous mask where it had gone through the flaming loft. But he still kept on coming.

Nolan knew he had one shot left as surely as he knew he was dying. He wanted to put the bullet in Kincaid and didn't care what happened after that. He owed that much to Harry.

He ran straight and fast on the blazing columns of his legs towards the wagon blocking the entrance to the burning stable. He hauled back the hammer of the long-barrelled Cavalry Colt. ready to blast the last shot of his life into Harry's killer.

He never got the chance because Kincaid lifted a Winchester off the tail of the wagon and pumped three shots in a tidy grouping through Nolan's chest. The Colt exploded upwards at the burning roof as reflex action tightened the gambler's finger on the trigger at the same time as he pitched backwards, lifted off his feet by the power of the heavy-calibre rifle.

He toppled over in a cloud of sparks that were immediately covered by the flaming bulk of roof timber that crashed onto his chest. Then one side of the loft toppled inwards, covering his body under a great mound of fire.

Behind the blaze, Jubal slid fast down the ladder. He hit the floor and powered himself over to the bonfire topping Nolan's corpse, the converted Colt was on the ground to one side and he picked it up as he tried to spot Kincaid. He couldn't see Mary's killer, but two shots told him the man was still there. He blasted two shells through the flames in reply and then ran

123

back towards the far end of the stable.

The tow-headed kid smelled a whole lot worse with fire adding odour to his natural putrefaction, but the rear end offered Jubal his only chance of escape.

He hit the burning wall at a run, powering his lean body through the timbers in a rising shower of sparks. The wood gave way beneath the impact and he crashed through into fresh air, blinking tears from his eyes as he rose to his feet. He cocked the Spencer and ran around the side of the building, triggering the rifle as he came to the front.

.30 calibre bullets raked the length of Kincaid's wagon as Jubal levered, squeezed, and levered again. He fired blindly, spreading shells along the length of the vehicle, blasting the thing apart in his need to kill.

But Kincaid was no longer there. Jubal heard the sudden thunder of hooves and looked round to see the scarfaced man hunched low in the saddle as he kicked a horse in a wild gallop down mainstreet. He dropped to one knee, resting the Spencer carefully against his right shoulder as he sighted through the smoke. The foresight was dead centre on Kincaid's back as the trigger dropped the hammer. Jubal felt the rifle buck hard against his shoulder as the cartridge detonated in the chamber. At the same time Kincaid jinked the horse to one side around a group of townspeople, so that the bullet missed him. Jubal saw a sack fall from the saddle as the gunman disappeared into the smoke and triggered two wild shots after the fleeing figure. If they hit, he didn't know, because Kincaid was gone, riding wild and free out of San Rafael, or what was left of it after the fire.

Cursing, Jubal looked around for a horse, but there weren't any, so he ran down the street after Kincaid. He stopped when he reached the fallen sack, realizing that the killer was too long gone to catch without a mount.

He lowered the hammer of the Spencer and lifted the sack. It was heavy, and when he opened it he saw the dull yellow of gold. He wasn't sure exactly how much the poke was worth, but he reckoned it had to be around four thousand dollars' worth, so he hefted it over one shoulder and started looking for a horse.

The citizens of San Rafael stood aside as the smoke-grimed man walked purposefully down the centre of mainstreet, ig-

124

noring the smouldering wreckage to either side. They watched him walk through to the far end of the dead town and grab the first horse he found.

Then they stood silent as he mounted up and rode away towards the East.